# Pete and Alice in Maine

# Pete and Alice in Maine

**A NOVEL**

## Caitlin Shetterly

HARPER

*An Imprint of* HarperCollins*Publishers*

This is a work of fiction. Though there is a general tendency for a reader to say, when reading nonfiction, "That never could have been true," and when reading fiction to say, "This is all based on a true story," the reader would be in error, though it is fascinating to consider why this happens. All names, characters, places, and incidents in this book are products of the author's imagination or are used fictitiously and are not to be construed as real. Any resemblance to actual events, locales, organizations, or persons, living or dead, is entirely coincidental.

For my Meme 1927–2022: ". . . to have been loved so deeply, even though the person who loved us is gone, will give us some protection forever." —J. K. Rowling, *Harry Potter and the Sorcerer's Stone*

and

For my husband, Dan, who found time for me when there was none to find.

All that June the weather had mocked the Maples' internal misery with solid sunlight.

—John Updike, "Separating"


I used to believe in happiness. I did not understand that we never fully arrive in that universe. We visit for miraculous moments and then travel all the other universes.

—Meredith Hall, *Beneficence*

# 1

• • •

# Visible Holes

I'm not sure why this all appeals to me. Maybe I am, intrinsically, a lazy person and having a small circumference of space in which to tread and retread is somehow satisfyingly comforting; maybe I like doing away with grocery shopping—well, honestly, I hate grocery shopping—and ferrying my children to dance and piano and basketball and smiling at other mothers I have nothing in common with; maybe I like having those bastards at Amazon deliver my olive oil and flour and instant oatmeal and stamp pads for my youngest daughter, Iris, to stamp rainbows and moons all over the bathroom walls, which makes Pete yell and then me yell and then Iris cries while Sophie says something caustic to all of us. Maybe I like the feeling of being on an ark—an ark that, at least for now, has no visible holes.

Maybe I like things simple, confined. Or maybe it's just that this way my husband can't leave me.

But. Anyway.

We came up here to escape, to shelter. I half expected armed guards at the border, not letting us across the Piscataqua Bridge. I thought we'd have to swim. Or go back. Or get stuck in New Hampshire forever; we'd be forced to live free or die.

But there were no guards, just a quiet I-95 and the sign WEL-COME HOME. Is this *our* home? It's our second home, in July and August. We pay taxes. And I certainly enjoy the gray-shingled simplicity of our low Cape and the thick, bristly lawn around it, the waves hitting the orangy-pink granite rocks at the end of our yard and then the ocean beyond roaring through stormy nights. But until now, it wasn't home, really. We called New York home. This was just another appendage of our luck, this place. And it still is. But like Job's messengers, we got out.

That isn't the important part of why I am telling you this, though. I took a writing workshop in Saratoga one summer taught by a writer named Lee K. Abbott. He's dead now. Doesn't surprise me—guy was a drinker and smoker and to be around him was like playing with a top that's spinning out of control in the most extraordinary and exciting way. He wrote one of the best first lines to a story. I don't remember the name of that story now, but I'll never forget his words: "I would not want to be one of those memoirists who begin a recollection by saying, 'Attention, people, there's a dead dog in these pages,' but alas, I am and there is." When I start writing a story—or, when I used to, back, before—I'd think, Where's my dead dog? Should I tell them about the dead dog?

Anyway, that's not important either. Sorry. I'm digressing. Our privilege is clear, almost criminal. I am reminded over and over of this fact as Iris screeches about Sophie stealing a Lego and then hits her and Sophie pushes her back against the hardwood floor and Pete raises his voice and doors get slammed and then pancakes still somehow appear on our breakfast table for us all to enjoy, even if both girls have sour expressions on their faces. We are here; we can shelter together, we can drive each other crazy, we don't need personal protective equipment; no one is counting on us to save their lives. We must only save our own.

That is the story.

We got here late at night on a Wednesday. Schools had closed. It was already bad; panic had seeped into every corner of the city, and in the evenings the rats were out, moving like gray-black shadows through the eerily empty streets. Getting into the elevator felt like walking into a war zone. Picking up the mail was dangerous, maybe suicidal. New Yorkers were all scared of one another. For those few odd days when we waited for the tsunami but our lives still went on and school was still open, I was scared of my own children, I was scared of Pete coming home from work; I didn't want him touching me or the girls in case he had it. Every throat clearing or sniffle elicited a code orange.

"We can leave," I told Pete the Sunday before we did. We were in bed. It was after midnight. Not since 9/11 had I heard ambulances punctuating the night like this. I couldn't read, I couldn't leave the bed, I couldn't sleep. The sound had me frozen in some sort of PTSD time warp. "We don't have to stay."

"You want to go to your parents?" he asked. I could tell he meant just me and the girls. He'd stay and man the fort, stoic as this was of him. We females would go to Minneapolis and hunker down, he was thinking.

"No. Maine," I said.

"The house is shut down," he countered.

"I know."

"And it's still cold. We have no way of heating it. We've used that fireplace in the living room—what, once?—and the whole house filled with smoke. The pipes will freeze once we get the water on."

"We'll buy an electric heater or two. Look at the map on the *Times* site: they don't have any Covid up there."

"Or any that they know about. The testing, Alice. It's bullshit."

"We should go. It's safer."

"I still have my job." Yes, the job. The problem of the job. The job that has supported us and allowed me to be a mother and chief officer of: the Calendar and the Laundry and the Spare Clothes Bags for school and all the Camp Forms and all the Doctors' visits while Pete works. The job that gives me "time" to try to be a writer when the girls are in school, if I can think of something to write with the few brain cells I have left from being a mother; the "time" I use to fill notebooks with endless ideas for plays and stories and novels and TV shows—stacks and stacks and stacks of them that never get opened again and end up in a vinyl bin under our bed. The job that makes our money and is *the thing*, especially since Number Two, that ties us back together, over and over again, ever since he began *the other thing*.

"Tell them you'll work remotely."

"The country is headed for financial disaster. They'll need me here."

"They might not need you at all, Pete."

Silence. A mode he slides into effortlessly, with no idea that the girls and I are dangling on the other end of a rope. It can mean anger, or sometimes, just not knowing what to say. Sometimes he's just vanished. Where he goes in silence scares me. Then, after such a long wait that I thought he'd gone to sleep, he said, "We have no internet up there."

Right, I anticipated this: the problem of the internet. No internet was my requirement when we bought the Maine place, when Pete was on the rise and I could see I was losing him to the constant demands of his job, to the screen always in front of him, the Bluetooth in his ear, even at dinner. It's funny—what had initially compelled me to him, as soon as we'd had Sophie, became that which I wanted to excise from our lives: his hustling, trading, fast-talking, advice-giving, market-playing self. It was that person to whom the other men gave fist bumps when we arrived at a party; that smiling, confident energy that made other wives flirt with him; that person who talked deals all the way through a workout with his trainer at Equinox; that was my guy who got us to the front of the line at Nami Nori on a Thursday night.

Pete *is* magnetic, hard to resist, and exciting—the very qualities I thought would carry us both, fueled on his energy alone, into a life of success. But when Sophie came, I got stuck. I wanted to make cookies like my mother used to; I wanted to make forts out of cardboard boxes and take long walks in Riverside Park and wear sweats all day. I still wanted to write; but the career I'd been slowly building with a poem in a journal here, a story in another journal there, one little three-person off-Broadway play that got a notice in a longer review of "Ten Young New York City Playwrights to Watch" in the *New York Times*, no longer felt imperative. Everything I'd learned in college and in the acting, playwriting, and directing classes I'd taken all over New York City, and what I'd learned just in rewriting and rewriting again, seemed to slide into the mush of the compost bin. Days and then months passed in the time it seemed to take for me to change a diaper. I could no longer triage my own thoughts, let alone my own needs; "Me" didn't even make the list. When we went to parties or took an Uber out to Brooklyn to eat at Red Hook Tavern, even if I'd put on my nicest dress, slimmest jeans, or sparkliest shirt, I often felt out of step with Pete. In my mind, I still had spit-up in my hair; I was still changing diapers and nursing. I wanted to be home with Sophie; I wanted to feel her soft skin and buttery smell; I wanted her hot cheek pressed against my neck, her drool dampening my collar. I wanted to go home and pry her from the arms of the nanny, whom I came only to resent.

It's such a tired story, but by the time I'd fired the nanny and required that our house in Maine be an oasis from everything in New York that was slowly swallowing my soul, Pete and I were no longer going clickety-clack down the same straight-line track. Our tracks merged for the girls, for the convenience of our lives, and we continued on, while I spent years of money and time in therapy trying to figure out how unhappy I really was and how much I loved him and whether I'd be truer to my most authentic self if I were able to leave him. Not because he did anything too terribly wrong, that I knew of—until he did. It was the feeling all the time that he might. Or might have already. Or that maybe *I* might, who knew? But I never got beyond just that one, agonizing question: *Should I?* I was perpetually treading water. I had lost my way in the world.

Gosh, had I disappeared for a moment like he does? Yes, it was the internet issue we were talking about. "We can install it, Pete. We will have to. And until they come you can go to the library in town. Your phone and iPad will work in the field. The whatever that is up in the sky that makes things like that work, will work," I said.

"It's the cellular network."

"Right. That."

Silence, again.

"When do you want to leave, Alice?"

"Now. Tomorrow."

"That's nuts. There's no way we can get us all out of here by tomorrow. It might not even be that bad. Right now might be the worst. We can sit this out."

"It's going to be that bad. We need to go. The girls. I'm taking them . . ." What I didn't say and he knew was: "You need to choose." My stuckness was unsticking. Action was rumbling inside me for the first time in years.

When he agreed, he wasn't choosing me. You get to a place in a marriage and you know that. He was choosing our girls, our black cat, Ingmar, and our shiny car, all over me. He was choosing the house in Maine over me, paid for by his gains while others lost during the Great Recession a decade ago, when being on the side that wasn't free-falling was a criminal advantage.

"You'll need to pack us up" was all he said. And then we lay there drifting in and out, listening to sirens alternate with silence, unable to turn to each other.

I don't know what they worked out for him. He said he was going to work from home. He'd use his phone and computer to manage his guys, analyze numbers, assess risks, send the bank's president his projections, lean in and away from trades, and pull strings that would affect the entire country, or world, even, just with the invisible wand he'd wave on his laptop. Did he tell The Her he was going? Did he say goodbye? Were there five of us, or more to the point, the germs of five times whatever other contacts we five had been exposed to, in the car when we left—fifty people, could it be? More? Does anyone know?

The sun was mocking us when we drove up the Hudson and north, as if this were all a figment of our imaginations; life was just fine. "Smile and go back home," the sunlight glinting on the river seemed to insist. When we got in the car, I'd said, "We won't stop, girls. You each have a jar back there to pee in if it gets desperate. When we get farther out, we'll stop on the side of the road."

"What if I need to poop?" asked my five-year-old, Iris, her

brown hair falling straight and soft, like a pelt, and framing either side of her pointy white face, her green-and-copper-flecked eyes trained on mine.

"You'll try to hold it," Pete said, his hands gripping the steering wheel tightly, his knuckles cracked dry from so much sanitizer and handwashing. Something about his dry hands steering us away from the chaos of New York stirred a feeling of love in me I hadn't felt in a long time. Instead of fury and shame that I couldn't manage to leave him after years and years of thinking I'd be happier and saner if I did, I felt safety and comfort wash over me.

"For nine hours, Dad?" said Sophie. She sounded sarcastic with the tiniest hint of fear salting the edges, like a Ritz cracker.

"Maybe it will only be two by the time you realize," Pete offered.

"I hate you guys," she retorted and put her earbuds back into her ears, closing her eyes behind her big red eyeglass frames, her incipient eleven-year-old's breasts heaving on her chest as she let out an audible sigh to express how terrible we were. I handed Iris my phone so she could send me emails full of broken hearts and turd emojis and closed my eyes. I already needed to pee myself, but I'd have to wait until Rhode Island, when I could go in some woods, if there were any woods still left in the state of Rhode Island. Ingmar meowed in the back.

In our exodus, packed all around us, in the trunk and in our rooftop bin, were two jumbo boxes of kitty litter, Ing's litter box, the one twelve-pack of toilet paper I could find, four shrink-wrapped twenty-four-packs of Poland Spring bottled water, six bags of groceries from Fairway, a laptop for each of us, school-work, markers, No. 2 pencils, legal pads, jelly beans for Easter baskets, boots, and all the books I could fit.

I had packed every blanket we owned, every sweater and coat, all the socks I could find that matched, every hat, mitten, or glove in our apartment, and every pair of pj's. Though we'd owned the Maine house for most of Sophie's life, in the winter the contours of our second home and what was there became blurry for me. I could picture the summer light falling across the beds and the rumpled sheets and pillowcases; I could picture the inside of the old fridge that hummed in the kitchen all night long; I could picture the waves outside. But whether I'd left sunblock or bug dope, how many blankets there really were, and whether the old clothes of Sophie's I'd packed away in bins in the barn were going to fit my youngest daughter, these were things I did not know.

When we were in Maine for six weeks of every summer, my life felt borrowed. I never thought of any of it as mine. I hadn't grown up with two houses. That's not to say we were poor. My father was a podiatrist, my mother his receptionist. My parents worked hard to pay for our one low ranch outside of Minneapolis. It wasn't until I moved to New York that I realized what being wealthy could mean.

When Pete bought the house in Maine at the bottom of the market, he decided, ever the moneymaker, to rent the place for the first three weeks of July every year. "The house is better off making money for us than sitting empty," he said. "Plus, the renters will scare out the mice."

So, when the girls and I arrived each summer in late July, our things had been someone else's things, which added a layer of mystery and confusion to what was ours, what was constant, what needed to be unpacked and cleaned and found, even if I didn't remember ever having had it.

Many of the things in that house had been Pete's mother's, and before that, his grandmother's, sitting on dark, lacquered shelves in old stately homes in Westport, Connecticut. Silver and china I would not know was gone if the renters stole it. Yet I somehow always felt when I got to the house that it was my job to make sure these things I couldn't remember were indeed still there. Things and more things accumulated around us as our lives moved on, as our girls grew. When both Pete's parents died, more things made their way to Maine and into our apartment in New York, things I'd never seen before and had never tried, like a set of caviar spoons.

In summers, when we all were there, and had been at the shore picnicking and swimming, doing our best to be a family for the weeks Pete was with us, I would sometimes leave them and hike up the hill we called Christina's World to the house to retrieve a diaper, when Iris was small, or an extra Fresca, or the sunblock. I'd enter the cool house alone and it felt like I was visiting our lives; we were there but not there. From this distance I could see the clean lines of the rooms, the white walls and bookshelves lined with books, the vase of hydrangeas on the sideboard, the lucky providence of money.

\* \* \*

Poor Ingmar couldn't hold it. No one had told him he had to. Ingmar, an unseasoned traveler, got our apartment mostly to himself in summers when we were gone, visited only once daily by a teenage cat sitter from our building; now he had to come with us. At some point Iris went to sleep despite the car reeking of cat shit, despite the sloshing of urine in the canning jars both girls had managed to crouch behind the seats and mostly pee into, despite the dinner of cheese sticks and pretzels. I could hear an audiobook imperceptibly coming through Sophie's earbuds; her eyes were closed and her head lay back, but her body was tense, awake.

The night stretched long before me as I imagined the cold house, the tired girls, the mouse poop on counters, the entire container of baby wipes and six bottles of water I'd probably have to waste so that I could bathe our shit-covered cat, and the orange juice I'd forgotten to buy so that our first morning could be just a sliver sunnier.

In the dark, we finally crossed the bridge to Verona Island, the huge rocks along the side of the road impenetrable. We drove through Bucksport and turned right toward the Blue Hill Peninsula, finally making our way through the darkened town and out to the shores facing Deer Isle.

We pulled into our driveway, our tires crunching on gravel and hard snow. We drove up the short rise of a hill where we found our house looking just as it had when I first saw it: *The Little House* in the children's book by Virginia Lee Burton. But now, in the moonlight, I noticed that the house looked solemn and puritanical. Maybe it didn't want us.

Pete got out and unlocked the door, his skin pale against his dark hair in the frosty air. He went in and took a walk around to look for rodents and then came back out to grab some of the blankets I had packed and to tell me he was going to make up the beds. I sat in the car with the girls, watching the stars in front of me through the windshield.

Behind me Iris was breathing heavily in her sleep. Sophie shifted and cleared her throat. "Mommy?" she said quietly.

I turned back to her. "Hey, Pumpkin, did you sleep at all?"

"I don't know," she said, her voice groggy and her face soft. I could see the big blue-eyed baby I used to carry on my chest for long walks as she slept, her cheek mashed against my breasts. I wished for a moment that I could pull her onto my lap now and smooth her hair the way I used to, nuzzle her neck.

Instead I said, "We're here. Look at the moon!"

"The house looks different."

"You're just not used to seeing it in winter, without leaves and flowers." I noticed the shadows it was casting on the patchwork of frozen ground and thin white snow. They made the house look long, and the moonlight made it look white, even though it is gray-shingled.

Pete came back out and stood, tall and angular, looking around. Watching his quiet frame set against our house took me back more than one hundred years into an imaginary world inhabited by Ethan Frome–like characters.

He opened the car door quietly. "Hey, I'll take Iris in first. I've got her bed ready. Sophs, I'll come back for you, honey."

"Okay," Sophie said, still quiet and soft and vulnerable. Our baby.

"I love you, honey." He made eye contact with her.

"Okay," she said again.

Swaddling Iris in a blanket, he carried her in, her mouth open against his shoulder. I waited with Sophie.

"Sophs, put your jacket on," I advised.

"Okay," she said again, her acquiescence either telling me she was still half asleep or in some kind of shock.

When Pete came back once more, a woolen afghan in his hand, he opened her door. "Hey, sweetie. I know you're big, but just let me carry you in. I can take you upstairs and put you right into your bed."

"Okay, Daddy." I turned back to examine her, wondering if I could still see traces of the sullen preteen who had left New York with us.

Staggering slightly, he carried her long body to the door and disappeared inside.

This was the moment I had been waiting for. Alone, finally, I got out, the cold air hitting my face. I breathed in ocean and brown frozen ground and a darkness of secrets. "Hello, house," I said. "We are here. Please take us in. We need you." The house was silent, but not necessarily hostile to my request.

Pete came back out. "Number One's in bed."

"Is she asleep? She was acting weird."

"Nah. Just tired. She wanted her light on."

Together we unpacked the car and then, finally, Ingmar.

* * *

When morning came, Ingmar was still damp and angry, and the sky was gray with rain pelting the windows. Pete called Dale Carter to tell him we were up early and were opening the house. "We could use your help," I heard him say, "getting the water turned on and the hot water up and running through the old heater. We'll need the storm windows off and the boat from the yard." Pete had the phone on speaker so he could butter toast for the girls' eggs and soldiers.

Dale was silent on the other end. "You're up from New York City?" Dale asked, saying *York* like it was spelled *Yawk*.

"Right," Pete said. "We needed to get out. We needed to feel safe."

Silence again.

I could hear Dale shuffle and sigh into the phone. "You're not goin' to want those stoam windows off yet. It's only Mahch. Lotta wintah still comin'. Ain't Jew-lie."

"Okay." Pete was chastised. "Forget the storm windows."

"Forget the boat too. Boatyahd's closed."

"Okay."

More silence. Finally, Dale offered one more pearl: "Pete. Sorry to tell ya, but no one up heah is goin' to help ya. You'll need t' lay low, keep ta yoah-selves. Least till it's been the foah-teen days theyz talkin' about on the TV. I hope you brought some toilet paypah." He chuckled.

Pete said, "Oh." Just that. Just "oh," like someone had just slapped him in the face. Then, "Goodbye, Dale."

"Good luck to ya, Pete."

"Don't worry." He turned to me. "I can figure out the water. We'll be fine. I don't know why we paid someone else to open our house all this time anyway."

"Probably because we had renters? And then the girls and I were here alone in July? Should you find someone else?"

"I'll call the general store. Maybe someone there knows someone else who can help."

I stood listening while he dialed and the phone rang. He cleared his throat and asked, "Yes. Hello. We've just come up last night to our house here in town from New York. We need some help getting it all turned on—" Silence. Then, "Oh. Okay. Right. Yes. Thank you. Goodbye."

"And?"

"Guy at the store told me that no one's helping anyone from away."

"That's lovely. What is this, the Russian Revolution?"

"Anyway, it's not anything I can't do. I do have a few skills, Alice."

Not quite two hours later, we heard the chain saws. There's no sound quite like the finality, the heavy thud, of a tree going down. Then came another thud and the loud bang of limbs cracking. We all ran outside, looking around, not even sure which direction to go until we heard car wheels speed away and then raucous laughter and hooting echoing back to us. The driveway isn't long; a soft, dirt roll through a stand of old cedars and lilacs to a big old white pine that casts a cool shade in summer onto the main road, which is tar.

We could see immediately that, at the bottom of the rise, two of our trees were down: Our big, impressive oak that punctuates the right side of our field along the road lay spent across our driveway. Farther down lay our white pine; its crooked branches that made it look like a modern dancer swirling in the middle of a stage were now all akimbo on the ground. "All the world's a stage," I used to say to the girls every time we pulled in.

All four of us ran down the hill and stood together looking at the trees. No one was around. The trees seemed to be shuddering with their last breaths of life.

"Are we staying forever?" Iris asked, her eyes huge in her head.

"Do we even own a saw?" I asked Pete.

"I told you I thought we should stay in New York," he answered.

"You never said that. And besides, you had your own Goddamn reasons for staying. We should call the police."

"Ha, Alice, the police! Dale's cousin is Jimmy Eaton, a policeman, as you might remember. He's probably off duty today and came over to help in his flannel and work boots. I've told you this before—Maine is a lawless country; every local's got a gun in the back of their pickup. It's Texas with Bean boots."

"Guns, Daddy?" asked Iris.

"Great job, Pete, you're terrifying our daughters."

"No one wants to hurt us, sweetie. They just don't want us to make anyone sick with the virus," Pete offered Iris.

"Do we have the Corona?" asked Iris.

"No. Certainly not," he answered. Iris was barely listening to his answer. Distracted now by the trees, she was scrambling over their branches, which gave me a second to lash out.

"So, we've got two fallen trees now, no way to get out, every-one here hates us and thinks we have the f-ing plague, and we're standing here fighting and you don't think we should call the police. Awesome."

"Alice, just"—and he put up his hand to silence me—"stop screeching."

"Do *not* give me the Trump hand, Pete. And I am not screech-ing." I might have been, though.

"Jesus H. Christ, Alice! I knew this was a bad idea, coming to Maine. Fucking absurd." And then, shockingly, he kicked one of our trees. Or at least the branchy air around it.

Before I could comment on the obvious ridiculousness of whatever it was he just did, Sophie intervened.

"Guys! Stop it. Do we even have enough food?" My eldest daughter, Sophie, ever the pragmatist.

Before anyone could answer, Iris beckoned us over to the trees. "Look," she pointed. Spiked into our white pine was a piece of paper with black writing in Sharpie. Sophie read it out loud: "GO BACK TO NEW YORK. YOU'RE NOT WEL-COME HERE! THIS IS OUR HOME. DON'T MAKE US SICK."

I stood stroking the old white pine's bark and smooth, deli-cate needles. "I'm sorry," I whispered. "This is my fault."

\* \* \*

That was fourteen days ago. None of us has gotten sick, thank God. Pete did manage to get the water running, just as we ran out of bottled water. For the toilets we hauled cloudy, mossy water for a couple of days from the stream that gurgles through our property to the ocean. In the beginning, at night, I felt scared. Instead of the refuge I was expecting, we were hemmed in and that felt unsafe, wrong. We had exactly no one up here to ask for help. I wondered to Pete, "Will someone come hurt us since they know we can't escape?"

"Don't be ridiculous," he told me. "This isn't a Stephen King novel."

"That's not helpful."

"Look, it's dark and you get scared when it's dark out, Alice. Plus we're in the middle of nowhere. But no one is going to do anything to us. They were just keeping us in line. Martial law around here. Better to just do it. We're okay. We'll be okay."

Pete hasn't shaved since we got here, and his beard has come in curly and black, flecked with gray on his cheeks. I don't wear makeup anymore; I pull my hair back into a bun stuck through with a pencil. When we get cabin fever we go outside, bundled, and run up and down the driveway together. Gone are the days of the gym and PE. At night, I check the girls for ticks but let them go to bed dirty.

We've had no heat. The small amount of wood left over from last year went into the fireplace. We were done with it in three days. Then we wore sweaters and huddled together under blankets reading. We ran out of toilet paper in a week, what with spring runny noses, and both Sophie and I got our periods. Her first! Thank God it was light, almost inconsequential. I had thought to pack four boxes of pads when we left the city. She cried. More, I think, from the shock of seeing her own blood coming from down there. I showed her how to stick the pads into her underwear; I watched her grimace at the bulky feeling between her legs. I told her I hated it too, and that when she was a little older we could try tampons. When it was over in two days, I was relieved, grateful.

"But look at the bright side," I told her. "You don't have to wear these to school! I was exactly your age when I got mine. And going to school was the worst. I don't think my mother even showed me how to use a pad. I used to bleed through all the time into my pants and then I'd put a sweatshirt around my waist to hide it. I remember, once, there was a sticky patch of blood on the orange plastic seat at my desk. The point is, you get some time to practice—at home, with us, here. It's safe."

"Don't tell Iris," she made me promise.

"Don't worry," I said.

"Or Daddy."

"Daddy will want to know, honey."

"Okay. But not Iris."

"Deal."

For toilet paper, I cut up a pile of old baby clothes of Iris's I'd found in a bin in the barn and taught the girls to wet the final piece to make sure they were clean. I set up a plastic bag for soiled rags in each bathroom and washed them every night with hot water and soap.

The food I'd brought from New York—flavored cream cheeses and H&H bagels, pomegranate juice, chia seeds, and grass milk yogurt—lasted five days with everyone home and eating as much as we were. There's no Whole Foods up here, no grocery delivery service. So I quickly put in an order for everything I could find on Amazon that resembled actual food and tried to buy toilet paper but couldn't. UPS dropped the boxes by the felled trees and drove away.

We've been eating lots of jarred olives and big bowls of cereal with powdered milk on top. Out of habit, these are now the only two foods the girls want. The simplicity and expediency of cereal and olives, I admit, is freeing. It has been a welcome break from making school lunches and trying to figure out dinner back home. I've tried the odd baked thing with the flours that I can get online, after a long recipe-hunting session out in the meadow near the woods, where the reception is best. But my muffins haven't been nearly as successful as cereal and olives. Especially once the girls realized, after a first boring order of organic Heritage Flakes, that I was willing to order huge boxes of any junk cereal they could find on Amazon: Froot Loops, Cocoa Pebbles, Lucky Charms, Reese's Puffs, Franken Berry, miniature Twinkies cereal, Cinnamon Toast Crunch, Boo Berry, Honey Smacks, Trix, and even Drumstick cereal, which is made to taste like the little individually wrapped ice creams you get at the bodega. Do you realize that if you put "junk cereal" into your search engine you actually get junk cereal? Who wrote the algorithm for that? The girls couldn't believe I was willing to order those. Neither could I, honestly. "It's an anthropological study," I told them. "We will examine how insane you both get eating this crap for two weeks. My guess is that you'll never want a sugary cereal ever again."

"Ha, right. Iris will *never* go back to organic Leapin' Lemurs, Mom," said Sophie.

One evening, Pete was so desperate for something other than cereal and olives that he called the pizza shop in Blue Hill and asked if they would deliver to us out here if he paid extra. He offered a twenty-five-dollar tip. "No, they don't have the staff. Window pickup only," he told me.

Turns out you can order a chain saw from Amazon, but I think even Pete realized that chainsawing his way through two huge trees was beyond what he was capable of. We never tried. We knew that we needed to respect the local law; trying to bust out would only cement us as the pariahs we were already deemed to be.

Once, when we were outside, a truck went by and laid on the horn and someone stuck their head out and yelled, "Go home, you fuckin' out-of-staters!"

"They hate us," Sophie said, dropping her croquet mallet and going inside to disappear into her room.

"What did they say, Mommy?" asked Iris.

"Let's go make lunch," said Pete.

At some point in the midst of this, Sophie started having an imaginary friend again. Maybe that's a normal pandemic response in an eleven-year-old? Some regression has to be allowed for each of us, after all. This time her name is Collette and she is summoned in moments of stress, when Sophie wants to be dispatched as far away from her family as possible. "Collette and I are going to the woods. We will be back for dinner." I think she got the name from a volume of short stories on the shelf above the mantel. At first, Pete told her to cut it out. But when it persisted, we just learned to say, "Okay, see you both later." Kids need friends, after all. Does it matter if they are made of dreams and bones, as the song goes?

Despite the gray sky and pelting rain, small signs of spring arrived. Old bulbs I've never seen before came up around the lilacs—snowdrops and then bright yellow daffodils and then little blue flowers I don't know the names of and then the ones that look like deviled eggs. I saw the wild bees come out on warm days to drink water from damp spots, and I found an old book on the shelf about beekeeping that likely belonged to whoever owned this house before us. I began dreaming about keeping bees and planting a garden. Seeds for lettuces with wonderful names like Elf's Ears and Balady Aswan and Sweet Valentine and bush and climbing beans and pickling cucumbers and Harry Potterish–sounding Bellatrix pumpkins are now on their way, in the mail.

A week in, we dispensed with the presumption of school. Too hard to do on a phone while sitting in the soggy and cold meadow. Too hard, period. I let the kids run free so that I could read; anything, everything. The fatigue I suddenly felt once we were really and truly trapped was immense. Like weights on my limbs.

The internet people couldn't get in the driveway to set us up. And, without it, Pete couldn't be on the computer all the time as he had planned.

Without the tethering the internet would seem to provide for all of us, giving us online school, work for Pete, the news, and even recipes that are easily Googleable from within the warmth of the house, we have been in a constant free fall from hour to hour, morning to night, and then we start it all over again. I navigate my days in a dream state; everything seems fuzzy and without contours, and I'm not sure what is real anymore. When I get a signal on my phone, I hand it to the girls so that they can FaceTime with my parents. While they talk, I take a bath.

Pete put in a good few days bundled in a coat and hat and gloves trying to get a cell signal in the field, but it wasn't consistent and he couldn't get enough bandwidth to use his Bloomberg terminal out there. One desperate morning, he packed his backpack and said he was going to hitchhike to the library in Blue Hill and sit on the steps and use the internet there, because the library itself is closed. But no one picked him up. Of course: Covid. Four or five hours later, he came home. He said he'd sat outside in the cold near someone's house and used their unprotected wi-fi for a bit.

Now he's taken his vacation time. The CEO didn't love it. "Terrible timing," he told Pete. "What about this isn't terrible timing?" Pete groused. He blames me, I can tell. He doesn't say it out loud, thankfully, but I can see it hooded under his dark gray eyes.

But. In January, Pete had uncannily added the Clorox Company and more Amazon to our portfolio. So now, while we sit this out, we are getting rich. Is it wrong of us to be making money from all this? I know the right thing to say is yes. But even this fact, like everything else, seems fuzzy and stuck in some aspic in my brain, as if the virtual money we are making—off ourselves, even, as we buy everything we can on Amazon, Clorox included—makes no difference. We are still using rags to wipe our bums; we are still eating Cap'n Crunch for dinner.

"When this is over, when we can get out of here, we'll do something helpful with the money," Pete assures me, his wrists looking frail and hairy sticking out of an old flannel shirt he's been wearing to bed. Again, prickles of love stir in me when I see him soft and up close like this. At home in the city he's always walking out the door, always in motion. Here, he's stopped. I have him to myself. I can look closely and examine.

At night it is quiet. The girls, thin and lithe from eating cereal and olives day in and day out while running unbridled through the brown grass and woods and down to the ocean and back up again, fall asleep quickly. Some mornings we find Iris splayed across our feet hugging Ingmar, her breath hot and her body cold to the touch. Even though I sometimes am hungry and restless in bed, I feel safe. I know we are together. Those trees at the bottom of the driveway hold us in. That is their parting gift.

Last night, on our thirteenth night, Pete said in the dark, "Tomorrow, I'll call Dale and ask him to tell whoever cut those trees down that it's over. To come let us out. They've made their point."

"And then what?"

"What do you mean, Alice? We go get food. Buy toilet paper. Clean ourselves up. Then we get back to our lives. I'm done with Maine."

For a quick second, an image of our city bedroom with its pale lilac walls and the window that opens to the back courtyard of our building came into my mind; the magnolia blossoms in spring, the way I love looking out beyond them to the Hudson and over to Jersey. I shut my eyes tight. "I'm not going back."

"Ever?"

"No."

He was silent then. He knew I didn't just mean New York. I meant all of it. In this quiet, in this time of being stuck on our little rise overlooking Eggemoggin Reach, I had realized that I didn't need to go back, that I didn't need my life there to recommence. As miserable as being held prisoner like this was, something was shifting inside me; some schism was occurring.

"You can go once they let us out, Pete. Back to your job, to our apartment, to The Her. You can have it all."

"You realize that sooner or later all those people from New York and Massachusetts will come here too. The virus will come. Nowhere is safe."

"That may be. But right now, this is *safer*."

"What about the girls?"

"They will stay."

I could hear Pete breathing and outside the window I heard an owl call. The moonlight peeked through the curtains and our white sheets glowed in the dark. After a long time, I felt Pete's hand take mine under the covers.

In the morning I woke up to the sound of chain saws and men talking. When I got out of bed and looked out the front window, there was a car-size hole cut through the trees. We were free now. Anything could happen.

# 2

• • •

# Jingle and Go

April comes and I never like it. Back when I was a girl in Minneapolis, there was something about the snow dissipating to reveal the bare ground littered with trash and brown leaves and the bones of small creatures that didn't make it. Then there was the hungry desperation of the animals that *did* make it only long enough to end up as roadkill—their soft, furry bodies curled next to clumps of daffodils at the edge of someone's lawn, or under a hedge of forsythia, planted as a beauty strip on the side of the highway. My grandmother died in April; my college boyfriend broke up with me in April; my cat, Gretel, died in April; Pete's dog, Finn, the big old black Lab he had when we met, he also died in April; my friend Maeve's baby died in utero in April; she was two weeks away from delivery. This year, Covid's not over in April, even though our president said it would be. April, as T. S. Eliot said, is the cruelest month.

But on this day in April, we are free. And we're driving in the car into Blue Hill, everyone together, and for the first time we are going somewhere, anywhere. The plan is to pick up premade food at the Co-Op—this seems like such an incredible luxury—and then take it and go hike Blue Hill Mountain. We are all giddy at the prospect: Sophie remembers they have tapioca pudding in little plastic cups; Iris wants a root beer; Pete wants "half a cow" on bread; and I remember this tempeh Reuben I had last summer that was divine, or in my memory, after all that cereal, it seems like it will be manna from the gods. I am so hungry for food and life and people and a store that I am shaking with excitement. I know I will have no self-control and will buy everything in the store while also trying to be as fast as possible because of the virus. After we hike, the plan is to go to the Thai restaurant and pick up takeout for tomorrow's lunch and then go get three pizzas (yes, three!) at Barncastle and bring them home for tonight. No one could decide whether we wanted pizza or Thai tonight, so this is the "best of both" accommodation.

We have all the windows open and back home we have daffodils on our dining table. Our hair is flying around and Pete has found some old Maine license plates in the barn that belonged to who knows who many years ago, and he's got them on our car so we can go into town incognito. "Jesus, we might get shot at with New York plates," he joked to me in the morning.

"Shhh. The girls. You'll terrify them."

This morning, he's got Ryan Bingham on the stereo playing

"Jingle and Go," and Pete and I are singing along and laughing and leaning into each other when we sing the refrain, "Oh, you know / That's how I jingle and go!" Sophie is yelling at us from the back seat to shut up, but she's laughing and Iris is kicking against Pete's seat in her hiking boots and Pete isn't yelling at her because we all are having fun. I lean back and sing loudly to Sophie, "My Cadillac is cherry / My boots are crocodile . . ."

"Alice, you're stupid and you can't sing and you guys are both just idiots," she yells back at me over the music and the wind, but the smile on her face is the thing, the thing I hold on to. That's my sweet Sophie before she was a preteen, before Iris, before Maine, and Covid and Pete and The Her, before she grew up too fast in the last six weeks. Her happiness is infectious and Pete reaches over and moves a bit of my hair that's blowing into my face and ever so softly touches my cheek with the outside of his knuckle. "I love you," he mouths, and, "You're beautiful," and then he smiles his broadest, most magnetic smile, the smile that makes me weak at the knees, even now, even after everything.

I met Pete in April. Fourteen years ago. That rattled my theory that April was a month to buckle in and hold on tight because bad things happen in April. It's weird, but when I remember meeting him, I recall first this T-shirt I had back then that I was wearing that day: it was this super-soft American Apparel, almost see-through material and was a gray blue that perfectly matched my eyes. It had a deep scoop neck that came right to the top of my breasts. I've lost that T-shirt—maybe I left it in a washing machine somewhere in Manhattan; maybe it got stuck forever in the pocket of a gym bag that has since gone to Goodwill. When I met Pete, my hair was down, I remember that; in those days it was so long it almost hit my butt. "The color of a wheat field," a woman I knew from the theater told me. She was from the Midwest, so I believed her.

It was a warm day and I was at the dog park with a blue heeler named Sappho I was dog sitting. Sappho's owner, Lynn, was an intense and extremely intellectual documentary filmmaker whom I met at Starbucks one Sunday morning. She had dark hair and glasses and an unnerving gaze. We were sitting next to each other on barstools, looking out at the street. She spoke first. I still had a stamp on my hand from a Lucinda Williams concert at Irving Plaza, and she told me she'd been there too. We started talking about that show and then where we lived and my apartment and my roommates. It was years later when I remembered her and looked her up on Google that I realized how important she was; that she'd won an Academy Award for Chrissake. She asked me what I did and I told her I was a waitress. She snorted and said, "No one's just a waitress in New York City, let alone someone like you. What do you want to be?"

"What I want to be is a writer. I mean I am trying to be a writer. Sort of."

"You're a writer. No 'sort of' about it," she said. "What kinds of things?"

"Poems and stories. I wrote a play. It did okay."

"Do you like dogs?"

I said yes and she asked if I wanted a gig walking her dog, Sappho. *Walking* would be an understatement for what Sappho needed. She needed a ten-mile sprint every day. I'd pick her up at seven a.m. and put on her leash and off we'd go, running through Riverside Park like two banshees out of hell. Eventually, Lynn had to go away for filming and she asked me to stay with Sappho for a week. That first morning, a Sunday, I woke up to Sappho standing on my chest, her jaws as big as a wolf's, an inch from my face. She was panting.

That was the morning I met Pete. I'd thrown on that T-shirt and jeans and sneakers and slipped the leash on Sappho, telling her that we were going to the dog park and she'd have to behave because I was too tired to run her, and she'd also have to wait while I got a coffee. We hit the diner on the corner and then went down to the dog park. I let her go but kept my eye on her because sometimes she could be a nuisance. I was sitting on a bench and drinking my coffee out of one of those gold-and-white New York City paper cups and watching Sappho run around with a little white thing the shape of a watermelon, when this guy sat down next to me and unleashed his black Lab into the park. He had rumpled, dark hair and a crease on one cheek from sleep. He wore an expensive-looking navy blue T-shirt and Levi's. He had a cup of coffee in his hand—Starbucks—and a day's worth of stubble.

"Morning." He smiled a wan, half-awake smile. And then took a sip of his coffee as if it were whiskey and leaned forward with his elbows on his knees, which made the arms of his T-shirt slide up and expose a smooth, tanned bicep muscle with one tiny brown mole just before the arm curved back toward his chest. I couldn't take my eyes off his arms. They were so sensual and male and taut.

I was sure I had no chance. No makeup, half awake, bad breath; guy like that had women throwing themselves at him. Even so, I asked, "What's your dog's name?"

"Finn," he replied, not looking at me, taking another sip of coffee. "Yours?"

"Oh, she's not mine. She's this woman's. I'm dog sitting."

"Which dog?" He squinted into the dog park.

"She's that blue heeler over there. Oh, fuck, she's cornering that poor Pomeranian. My God, is she humping the poor thing? I'll be right back. Sappho, Sappho—no! Sappho. Leave that dog alone." I scanned for the Pomeranian's owner and a look of outrage, but the owner must have been one of the three women in the corner wearing sunglasses, tight jeans, and high-heeled boots; they were deep in a conversation and not paying attention. I sat back down next to Pete who I didn't yet know was Pete.

"Sorry. She can be a menace. She needs a real run. But I needed a coffee."

"I think Sappho lives in my building. Riverside and Ninety-Third? Finn will rough her up, won't you, Finny?" Finn did not look like a dog who would rough up anyone. In fact, he was strangely subdued, like a shy child who couldn't manage to leave his parent's side on the playground. Pete who wasn't yet Pete pulled out a tennis ball he had crammed into his jeans pocket and showed it to Finn. "Go get it, Finny," he said and threw, that arm muscle bulging like a bolt sliding into place. I sat back down and tried to watch Sappho. Please ask my name, I begged the gods.

Nothing. So I spoke, but way too late, as if it were some weird delayed reaction. "You live on the park there? Joan of Arc Park? I always loved that statue. I love that play! The line about having no eggs and a thousand thunders always makes me laugh. Don't kids sled around there in the winter?" God, Alice, SHUT UP.

"They sled. I don't know that play."

"Shaw. George Bernard Shaw. Don't worry. Sort of obscure. I mean, not obscure to people who know theater. But obscure to other people." Oh my God, I was melting. This was mortifying.

"Got it." He smiled and our eyes connected for longer than a second. Pete's got a megawatt movie-star smile that's ironic around the edges, and eyes that are so gray they are almost lilac-colored.

Is it possible he doesn't think I'm an idiot?

"Go get it, Finn." He threw the ball for Finn. Those arms! Finn was only interested in the ball. Not in the least interested in Sappho, who was making chaos in the corner by now wrestling with a tufted white-and-shaved-to-pink-skin poodle. They both were getting all dirty and the poodle's owner was on her way over, snapping her leash. I wanted to hide. "Sappho, please be normal," I whispered to myself.

Meanwhile, Finn got the ball, came back to Gorgeous Arms Who Has Never Read a Play and Probably Doesn't Read at All, and dropped it, saliva-covered, in the dirt and stood panting. This was a dog who knew one word: *ball.*

"You say something?"

"No, just talking to Sappho. I need to get her out of here. She's trouble. Maybe I'll see you in your building."

"Yeah, take it easy." That smile again. I'm going to do something ridiculous like trip right now, I thought. I went to Sappho, who was covered in dirt and grinning like Jack Nicholson. I clipped her leash on and walked across the stage of the dog park, trying to look graceful while being pulled by Sappho, who had now decided she was dying of thirst and needed to get to the water bowls by the gate in record speed. She was tugging and gasping and hacking like she had emphysema. After I stood there with my back facing Pete for what seemed like forever, I waved goodbye and Sappho and I headed out, starting to walk down the park and back to Ninety-Third Street. Like Orpheus, I made the mistake of looking back. Not Yet Pete was standing up, his Levi's hanging off his hips, revealing a glimpse of a red boxer short. When he leaned down to put Finn's leash on, I saw skin. For a second I was transfixed, and then I remembered myself and turned and started trotting down the park, back to the safety of Lynn's apartment. It was enough to be trying to be a writer in the city; adding a hot guy to the mix would only make my life more complicated.

But Monday night, I was waiting for the elevator after picking up some food at D'Agostino's to make dinner and Not Yet Pete came into the building carrying a basketball. He was all sweaty and had a duffel bag thrown over his shoulder. He was talking to the doorman, Ralph, and saw me.

"Joan of Arc!" he called as I willed the elevator to hurry up. "Hold the door!

"Thanks." He grinned as he ran up.

"How are you?" I asked. Be normal, I told myself. Don't

act like you're in the elevator with Ryan Gosling. He had a picture on his T-shirt of U2 and he was wearing red basketball shorts and neon Air Jordans and his dark hair was all curly with sweat.

"Pete." He stuck out his hand.

"Alice." I shook it and felt electricity go through my body and down into my nether region. I could smell his sweat mixed with a musky deodorant.

"Hey." He smiled again, still gripping my hand. I looked down at his hand on mine, and he said, "Oh, sorry," and he let it fall.

"This is me," I said and got off on the third floor.

"Good night."

"Bye." I turned to wave. Then I ran into Lynn's apartment and shut the door, gasping for air when I was inside. "Oh my God, oh my God, he is so hot," I screeched to Sappho, who met me at the door. The doorbell suddenly rang behind me. I opened it and Pete was standing there. Oh my good God, had he heard me? My face flushed red and I started sweating.

"Hey." He was smiling. "What time do you walk her in the morning?"

"We run. At seven."

"How about I come get you at seven? Finn and I will run with you. We can get coffee after."

God, he was so confident I would say yes. I said yes, but wished I had the ovaries to say no and make it a little harder for him. He looked like the kind of guy who got what he wanted with women. Oh, whatever! Let him get what he wants, I thought.

I barely slept and at six a.m., when Sappho woke me up by standing on my chest and breathing on me, her canines grazing my cheek, I almost didn't mind. I had hand-washed (forget meeting him in the laundry room) my nicest spandex shorts and my favorite ribbed tank top and a periwinkle sports bra that squished my breasts together nicely, showing just a bit of cleavage over the top of my tank. I pulled my hair back into one long ponytail and was just tying my shoes when the doorbell rang.

"Hey." He smiled, hair tousled.

"Hi."

Dogs sniffed, Finn drooling everywhere. Pete was wearing a black muscle shirt. I could see that mole.

We got downstairs and another doorman, Tito, was on duty. He opened the door for both of us and I caught him winking at Pete.

"Where do you want to run to?" Pete asked.

"Through the park, up to Columbia, or Morningside. I mean, do you have a job?"

"I've got time today."

"Okay, I like to run to Morningside, do a little loop around the ball fields in there, and then back."

We started running, Finn discreetly pulling at his leash, while Sappho was racing the Iditarod with me as her sled.

"You work?" he asked, as we ran.

"I waitress," I panted.

"Where?"

"French Roast."

"Just so you know, I read *Man and Superman* in a freshman Lit class. It was decent. What else do you do?"

"I write. I am trying to write, I mean. Jesus, Sappho! Slow down! But."

"But . . . what? Books?"

"But, I guess, I mean, I'm just writing stories right now. I wrote a play. You?" Let us please change the subject. I could smell his deodorant and it was making me light-headed.

"I work in finance. On Wall Street."

"Got it." I had nothing to say to that since I knew nothing about finance.

"Are you from Manhattan?"

"God, no, Minneapolis. You?"

"Westport. Connecticut." I'd never been to Westport. But there were girls I knew in school from Westport. And all that conjured at that point was a vague image of an immaculately set table, like the little drawings in the Miss Manners book my mother referenced when I was growing up.

Finn continued to plod neatly along, true to his master as we ran. Sappho, on the other hand, had become a deranged hyena on the end of my leash. She was darting here and there after every squirrel or dog that she saw or smelled, and I was running in circles. "You want me to take her?" Pete asked.

At first I said, "No, I've got this." Then two seconds later, Sappho pulled me off my feet, and when he helped me up he just carefully took the leash out of my hands and handed me Finn's leash. Finn was a dream to run with: smooth, dependable. I tried not to laugh as Sappho gave Pete a hard time, bounding all over the place. He had the leash shorter than I had had it and his gorgeous, glistening arm was tensed. By the time we got to Morningside Park, we were both laughing and he was furious at Sappho too. "She's nuts," he told me.

"No kidding." I was doubling over and almost peeing my pants.

We walked then and after a while we ended up at the Hungarian Pastry Shop, and Pete found us a table outside. We ordered coffee in the sun and we each got a croissant. We talked about our parents and college and about books and landed on *The Da Vinci Code*, which we had both just read. Then we talked about music and Ryan Adams, whom we both had seen in concert but at different times and in different places. The sun was shining and this guy could talk forever and even though I had been worried he had nothing to say of substance and he was all looks and that's it, he was not, he was blessedly not. At our ankles, the dogs were lying down, pooped, their leashes slack, and we were smiling and getting seconds on coffee and suddenly I felt like this was the first day of the rest of my life.

\* \* \*

Lynn was coming back on Saturday and I hadn't seen him again. I didn't have Pete's number and he didn't have mine. I hadn't seen him in the lobby or the elevator or the laundry room. I saw a dog walker take Finn out on Tuesday afternoon when I was on my way home from lunch with a friend. My heart was in my throat when I waitressed Wednesday night, but I was grateful for the mindless task. I did a lunch shift on Thursday and came back to shower and put on old sweats and a T-shirt and try to will myself to forget him.

At around nine p.m., there was a knock on my door. I opened it and there he was. Holding flowers. Pale yellow tulips. He was wearing a dress shirt and blue suit pants, like he was on his way home from work. I could smell his musky smell.

We stood awkwardly in the doorway while I thanked him for the tulips. I tried to stay removed. Then he said, "Sorry to drop out on you. I had to take care of something. Dinner tomorrow night? I've made us a reservation. If you're free. Which I hope you are. Are you?" He smiled and his grin was at once cocky and also the tiniest bit hopeful.

"Okay," I said, smiling. I was quickly trying to think of who I could get to cover my dinner shift at French Roast.

"Cool. I'll get you at eight?"

I shut the door and was leaning against it holding the flowers and trying to breathe when the doorbell rang again and I opened it and there he was and he said, "I can't wait until tomorrow. May I kiss you?" I think I nodded or laughed or who knows if I just stood there, but clearly I didn't resist, because he leaned in, over the threshold, and took my face in his hands and kissed me long and hard and before I knew it, his hand was under my T-shirt and he was inside Lynn's apartment and Sappho was jumping all around us and we were on the floor and we were laughing and then our clothes were coming off and he was pulling out a condom from his wallet and asking me if it was okay and then he was inside me and we were both breathing hard and it was all over in five minutes. And then he was lying on top of me and he was laughing, which made me laugh.

When we sat up, I was reaching for my T-shirt to cover up and he said, "Hey, wait. Stop right there. My God, you look just like that famous Botticelli of Venus with your hair hanging over your breasts like that. You are beautiful." I must have made a silly face because he asked, "Do you even know how beautiful you are?" And then he leaned in and kissed me so tenderly I felt like I might melt.

After we were dressed he said, "Now we can relax at dinner tomorrow. See you at eight." And he was gone, into the elevator and up to the ninth floor, where he said his apartment was. Where ours now is. "Oh my good God," I said to myself.

All day Friday I was sure I would never see him again. But at 8:05 p.m. he was at my door, this time with one bird of paradise. I left it in the sink and he shepherded me out of the building, his hand on the small of my back, and we got into a cab and went to Nobu, where we drank wine and ate fried rock shrimp.

*　*　*

I'm remembering all this in the car in Blue Hill when Ryan Bingham starts singing "Lover Girl" and I get quiet. "Can I take you out on the dance floor? / Can I take you and spin you 'round? / Oh, be my lover girl / Oh, be my lover girl." Whenever I hear this song, I think back to when I was younger and that first week with Pete and how fast everything went and those few days when he vanished and reappeared and I always ask myself, Should I have trusted something that tumbled that fast into an attachment? I went so quickly from the steadiness of the world I was chiseling away for myself, to the neap tide of Pete and the world we started making together.

When I told my mother I was marrying Pete, she didn't answer. I thought maybe the line had gone dead. "Mom?" I said.

"We don't even know him" was all she said.

"You'll love him," I told her. I was never sure that actually came true. But. Nevermind.

Today, everything is good, it's all working out. We're together again even though we haven't fixed or healed anything, we are laughing, we don't have Covid, we've busted out of jail, and there's still that sparkle between us. We pull into the Co-Op and Pete smiles at me and puts his hand on my knee, a reassurance of his love for me with this song as our soundtrack. He used to joke, before everything, that if he were ever to lose me, it would be to one of the "Holy Trinity of Ryans": Ryan Adams, Ryan Gosling, Ryan Bingham. Though obviously, Ryan Adams kind of fell off that list.

When I finally get into the store, I almost don't know what to do with myself. I am in my own bubble: the *New York Times* is telling us to wear masks, so I've got a pink bandanna of Sophie's around my face and a hand sanitizer in my pocket, a cart in my grip. I pile everything I can think of into it: tapioca and chips and sandwiches and root beer and tea boxes and freshly ground coffee and instant oatmeal and nuts and cheeses and fresh fruit and fresh vegetables—Hallelujah, vegetables!—and frozen vegetables and bread and peanut butter and jelly and sliced meats and a whole chicken and hamburger and a steak and wine and spices and flours and sugar and bacon. It's as if we've been on a desert island talking to a volleyball and eating coconuts for four straight years. I want everything.

I find a woodsy-smelling shampoo, if my nose through an old bandanna can be believed, and a conditioner that smells like lemons and body cream that smells like vanilla and cinnamon, and bath salts that are lavender scented, and soaps that are made with tea tree oil. And as much toilet paper as I can fit in the undercarriage of the cart.

When I come back out, my cart piled high with all that good food, Pete and the girls open the windows to the car and cheer. I blush and suddenly wonder if someone in the parking lot will recognize us as the people who were locked in, if we have a scarlet letter somewhere on our chests, despite the old license plates with the silly, tiny lobster on them.

The girls lean over the seat back and reach out to touch the brightly colored packages of frozen foods as I carefully pack them into the coolers we keep stored in the barn for boat trips all summer long. They watch and chatter as I nestle the milk in between frozen peas and sweet corn. I pile blocks of sharp and mild cheddars and mozzarella and jack cheeses on top of glass jars of local yogurt and the chicken and hamburger. Iris rubs her hands together with glee and says, "Oh, Mama, you got so much yummy stuff!" I put the thin package of bacon on top of it all and close the top firmly. I root around to find the sandwiches, chips, root beers, and a cold brew for Pete.

No one can wait for a picnic on the top of a mountain. We

tear open our food the moment I am back in the car and start eating immediately, our windows open, the radio off. The food tastes so good and the sun is so bright that I willfully push away every thought that threatens to bring me back into anger or doubt. By the time we get to the trailhead, Iris is practically drunk from the food and the sugar in the root beer, and I'm sure she needs to pee. She's trying hard to drive Sophie crazy, which Sophie always always *always* falls for. Iris has reached back into her memory and starts screeching out the window that Sophie is going to marry a boy named Josh back home in New York and then she takes a pickle that came with her sandwich and throws it at Sophie and yells, "I'm going to marry you, Sophie. I'm going to marry you. That's your ring!" Peals of insane laughter.

I look back, trying to keep my own face straight, and Sophie looks at me pleadingly. "This is getting really strange."

Iris loves it! "I'm going to marry you, Sophie, I'm going to marry you, Sophie. I'm going to marry Sophie, Mommy!"

I'm expecting Pete to snap; he has almost no patience for this stuff. But, before he can, as soon as he has the car in park, Sophie has jumped out, no mask, and is already running away from us up the trailhead. "Sophie," I call. "You need a mask!" She doesn't listen. She is off. Iris is bouncing and clapping her hands and laughing next to my legs as I try to pull out water bottles and my backpack. "Pete!" *I* am the one who's worked up. "Go after her!!! Here's her bandanna. Go get her!"

"Relax," he says, with more than an edge, his eyes suddenly hard. "She will be fine." But he takes the red bandanna and puts on his own green one and off he goes. Happiness has dissipated into chaos; we will need to get it back now, that long retrieval process of being a family, where nothing gold stays as long as you want.

Iris and I find Pete and Sophie on top of the mountain, and we all drink water and I dole out a little chocolate truffle to each person. I propose a toast. I say: "Let's clink. We made it. How about everyone say the first thing they want to make happen in our lives in Maine now that we are free?"

Iris says, "Drive around. See stuff."

Sophie thinks and then says, "Snapchat with my friends."

I look at Pete and we both say in unison, "Get the internet connected!" It's been too hard and tiring trying to live "real life" without it. Plus, I'm hoping the girls will go "back" to school—online, that is.

We all clink our water bottles and look into the distance. And then it's all downhill after that and we get to the car breathless.

We pick up the Thai food and the pizza and by then everyone is sleepy but happy and Ryan Bingham goes back on and the CD picks up where we left off and the car fills with the smells of curry and ginger and lime juice and also pepperoni and garlic. As we go over the bridge at the Blue Hill Falls and watch the water all white and roiled up, I am wondering if it's doing that reversing thing it does, where the tide briefly goes both ways at once and Ryan Bingham is singing in his scratchy voice, "America, America, unload that gun. Save a daughter, save a son. Our bullets dress them up in blood." And we're all quiet for the rest of the way home.

# 3

• • •

# The Phases of the Moon

For their entire fourteen-day confinement, Pete went to bed late, after both the girls and Alice were already sleeping. The house was cold at night, and he piled on a hat and various layers of coats of different levels of thickness. When Alice asked him what he did all evening, before coming to bed, he couldn't tell her. He could *tell* her, but he didn't know how to explain where the hours really went. They seemed to evaporate into a morass of darkness. In truth, he'd been working—or trying to, at least, stay "au courant," as he did tell Alice, by going out into the field to catch a signal so that he could read emails and the news and look up averages—but that's not all of it. Before that, each night, he did do the dishes while she got the girls to bed. He picked up the various books and pillows and throws that always have a way of falling between the two blue velvet couches that face each other just off the kitchen island. He man-folded the blankets into small, tight, thick piles. He neatly stacked the books on the table, without artistry, but tidily, their edges all aligned. He said good night to Iris first, and then Sophie, and once the house was quiet, he went outside. He felt sneaky opening the door to go, like he could get caught. Each time, his pulse quickened, and he slid through the smallest opening he could manage and quickly clicked the door shut behind him.

Once in the field, he stood still to retrieve his email, and type back whatever short message he could before his fingers numbed or he lost the weak signal. Invariably, the whole process was ridiculous, infuriating. Despite the fact that everyone in his office knew he was stuck for a little while, on hold, as it were, with no internet, and dependent upon whatever cell signal he could find between parting clouds, his assistant, with little else to do with her life, continued to send him countless messages on Slack. Veronica: twenty-five, tall, dark-haired, exotic, gorgeous, Italo-Columbian-French-something, hired for him and his partner, Doug, to share and, since #metoo, strictly off-limits. Something about her off-limits-ness made her an added annoyance to Pete, almost an affront. Because he couldn't load Slack in the field, her messages came into his email full of green boxes and weird symbols made from emojis digested by an inarticulate algorithm that tried to translate her Slack program into clumsy text. He had to scroll down, excruciatingly, on the cold screen and wait for the whole clunky message to appear. English is Veronica's second, or maybe third, or even fourth, language, God knows how polyglot and overqualified this woman is, and so there were always benign mistakes. Pete could hear her voice, silken, slightly nasally, millennial-coy: Good morning, Peter, (":slightly_smiling_face:") David Brinklage & Co. are sending over some numbers (":fr::ok_hand:") for you approval. I'll forward link 4 spreadsheet. Hope you're hangin' in. We got this (":clap::clap::muscle").

And then, Good afternoon, Peter (":smiling_face_with_3_hearts:"). The White House has asked for some modeling (":star-struck::star-struck::star-struck:"). You on the committee. We need them next week (":pray:" ":fr::ok_hand:").

Outside, with no one but the moon listening, Pete said loudly, "Veronica, you're a total fucking idiot. What the fuck is up with the fucking heart emoji? I have enough on my plate, thank you very much. I don't need your millennial mindfucking breasts-in-my-face-bullshit right now. Just do your fucking job. Can't you write a fucking email without fucking emojis? You speak, like, ten languages and all you do is send emojis. Jesus Fucking H. Christ. I can't fucking be on a committee when I can't fucking get onto my terminal to look at the fucking models you total fucking idiot." Pete realized he sounded completely unhinged standing in the frigid air with a million layers on, scolding a high-heeled twenty-something back in the city. He typed back, aggressively, his fingers pinging off the screen like hail, Veronica: I am in Maine. I have no internet at the moment, as I believe I've told you. I am taking a little time. I can be on the phone call with the White House if you schedule it, but I will need you to copy and paste the numbers and text or email them to me for me to look at. Again, I cannot open anything that uses any more bandwidth than an email. I can't get on

Slack. In other words, no spreadsheets. Please stop sending me anything over Slack. Thank you. Peter Laughton. No emojis. The last name, unnecessary. But there was a formality to its flourish that Pete appreciated.

After the nightly torture of the absurd and annoying emails, Pete walked around the perimeter of the yard to unwind, his hands in his pockets. The stars were so bright most nights and the moon bigger than he'd ever noticed before, hanging like a pendant over the Atlantic Ocean. Not ready yet to succumb to the tensions of what lay inside, he walked up and down the driveway, his breath puffing out like smoke from a cigarette, his shoulders stiff against the cold.

Something in Pete's mind broke free as he walked, like an iceberg in melting waters, and suddenly there were two women: the one asleep inside his dark and strangely unfamiliar house, and the other he'd left behind in New York. Even with the nearer woman just inside, it was the one in New York whose body he was surprised to find he still craved. He should feel guiltier. But in the cold air, alone, he was finally, for the first time all day, able to let his mind wander, to relive and reexperience, to try to make some sense. He couldn't help himself from replaying, even as he told himself not to, how her body cleaved apart at his touch. How she'd allow him to do anything at all, her body his for the duration, making him feel that he was free-falling. In the dark, alone, on the frozen driveway, he felt his pulse quicken, his body ache for hers, and then, suddenly, he'd realize, with shocking clarity, that there was nothing there for him other than weightlessness. No smile, no turn of phrase, no cute morning hair, no deeper experience. All Pete's life there had been women for whom he wasn't sure he felt much of anything beyond desire and release. He had assumed that that was it, that that feeling signified love. Until he met Alice.

Finding Alice was like making some sort of grave rubbing with a thick charcoal pencil on thin, translucent paper; the more of those dark scratches he made on the sheet, the more interesting the little blobs of light and texture appeared, and the more invested he became as she came into focus. When they had sex, even years later, even when, eventually, they both had one ear trained for Sophie and then for Iris, and even with his knowledge that Alice was invested elsewhere, always, that her heart was split by shards of love for all of them and portioned off into the lists she made for groceries and to-dos, when they were done, Pete felt filled in a way that steadied him against the rushy feelings the city and all it had to offer created inside his chest.

But at some point Alice had turned away from him. That was the thought that preoccupied him more than anything out on the driveway those cold weeks of March when they first landed in Maine, and then were marooned. He wanted, night after night, to try to puzzle it through, find the precise month or year when he should have realized. What he came to, night after night, was not one moment at all, but an unnerving and elusive feeling that he'd missed a gradual slide away, and that it wasn't just him his wife was no longer connected to, but their entire way of being. And instead of doing anything about it, instead of asking questions, instead of being interested in who she was becoming, Pete had just beamed his charms outward, kept going.

Alice, of course, did not wait up for Pete at night when he took his midnight perambulations. No golden light burned in the upstairs bedroom window indicating that she was reading or writing a letter, folding laundry, making her lists. Instead it was dark and quiet, as if she had given up. He found himself looking up to their window and wishing for some sign, pleading that she might find a way to show him what could come next, that she could lead him to a track that made sense, that recovered things. But she gave him no such indication. Her body, once supple and warm and always present, the embodiment of home with her slightly milky smell, was now rigid and unfamiliar to him. Pete heard himself say out loud to no one but the leafless lilac bushes, "She doesn't like me that much anymore." And then he wondered, "Did she ever like me that much?"

Maybe, it occured to him, some of the things about himself that were always less than appealing had finally stacked up into an ever-growing "cons" list that had come to outpace the "pros." There were the lies he'd told, ever since the beginning, for one thing. Little things, like what time he'd left the office. Or telling her that the train had stalled and sat on the track for at least forty-five minutes, when it hadn't. She was desperate at home with two kids, and he sometimes—okay, often—took his time getting home, less than eager to jump back into the fray. Every so often, he stopped and got a beer when he emerged from the train, or just simply took his time walking home. Or the times, not many, just a few, really, that he'd bought himself a coffee and sat on a bench and drunk it when he was running out for bagels on a Saturday morning. Or bought himself a new pen when he was shopping, because of course he could, it was just a pen, but then, strangely, hid the pen from Alice, like it was something he'd get in trouble for, a small luxury he should have considered giving to her, the struggling writer. Or lunches out that he told Alice he had spent at his desk. And then, of course, the bigger lies that got them where they are now.

There was also his moodiness. At times, his temper could flare in moments of familial chaos. Chaos annoyed him. And when was the last time he'd asked her about herself? he wondered. Like truly asked her, *How are you doing?* Or, *What do you think about X?* Or, *What are you reading?* He must have asked these questions. But in the driveway, once he got through the swimmy memories of the exciting and illicit extramarital sex he'd indulged in, he wasn't sure he'd asked Alice much of anything in a long, long time. Perhaps, even, a span of time measured by months or more. Was that possible? No. Impossible.

Because he always apologized when she caught him out in a lie, or when she told him he'd been an ass, he felt somehow cleansed of his sins. But now, stuck in Maine, in that drafty house, imprisoned, he knew he hadn't noticed her recession, had not realized that she wasn't standing still, that somehow all those little things were adding up. With his affair and on top of that their Covid exile, it was possible, he realized, that the last bits of any shine had finally rubbed off his armor.

How to swim back was the thing that confused him. Can one swim back?

In the dark, the waves crashed against the shore.

After a while, each night, Pete let himself back inside the

house and turned the lights out. His eyes were accustomed to the moonlit world and he preferred to keep it that way. And then, for reasons he couldn't explain to himself, every night, he proceeded, as if he were searching though rubble, to climb the old white stairs with the burnished mahogany banister as quietly as he could and then hunt for his family in the dark.

He made the rounds, like the Tomten in that peculiar little book Alice's mother gave Iris. First he came down the hall that separates the two girl's rooms, the large Paris café mirror at the end, hanging over a small antique cherry table that Alice has always kept lovely in the summers, with a pottery vase filled with hydrangeas and black-eyed Susans. Beneath it, there is the little night-light that is bright enough to illuminate the entire hall. He pushed open Iris's door ever so slightly to stick half of his body inside. He needed to be careful because Iris is a light sleeper and most nights ends up in bed with him and Alice. Tonight her door whinges on the hinges, and Ingmar looks up from the end of the bed, his green eyes gleaming.

Iris lies in a tight little ball. Her hair is a rat's nest; since coming to Maine she won't let them brush it. Pete says to himself, We've been so lost in our own fog, we can't manage to fight her. The blankets are hanging onto the floor and only covering about a third of his daughter's body, just her shoulders and part of her back. The moonlight comes through the window as if to make up for the blankets, casting a frosty cloak over his daughter, illuminating her small, ever-so-fragile bare feet. In the afternoons, the sun sets outside her windows and the room comes awash in deep golden and pink light.

Iris holds Big Bear with both hands, tensed against dropping or losing him in the dark whirlpool of covers. Taking care not to touch the doorjamb with his body, Pete slides into Iris's room and pulls the covers up over his daughter. Ingmar jumps down and runs into the hall while Pete smooths the duvet with the cotton cover depicting a stream and a fox family, a bear, and a raccoon all happily doing their thing without a care in the world. Iris murmurs and turns over, one hand loosening on Big Bear. She smiles slightly, puffs her cheeks, makes a bubbly sound, and then goes back to sleep.

Back out in the hall, Pete sees his own reflection in the mirror and looks away, checking on the moon outside as if to ground himself. Then he slides into Sophie's room and hears her snoring, her head back on her pillow, her mouth wide open, her pink duvet cover still neatly pulled up as if she fell asleep before any thoughts occurred. In here, on the eastern side of the house, the moonlight slices through the room like a knife, one side half cast in silvery white light, the other dark. His firstborn, this sharp-tongued girl, already on the journey to becoming a woman. Pete feels sometimes as though he were standing on the outside, rather like watching a march going by on the street, and being stuck on the sidewalk, unsure of how to join in. What a mysterious process. She too, he realizes with a sinking heart, is inscrutable to him; she's become fuzzy. He's lost—has he ever had?—his connection to her.

Nothing to do here. She sleeps unaided.

Pete walks back down the wide, red fir floorboards, trying to navigate the places that are the most warped and creaky. He can now hear Ingmar scratching around in his litter box in the front hall and likely throwing all of the litter out of the box and onto the floor while making loud chortling sounds of accomplishment. "Ing!" he whispers, adding to the cat's noise.

Finally, Pete comes to stand in his own bedroom's doorway. Alice lies there on the bed, stiff, the white duvet cover with little blue flowers scattered over it wrinkled, and her face bathed in moonlight, making her look gray and ghostlike, older than he remembered. On the bedside table is a large yellow plastic pot of shea butter. Alice slathers it all over her cheeks and face and feet and legs at night, giving them an earthy, musty smell. Since coming to Maine, she doesn't wear makeup anymore. In her hands, as she sleeps, is an old baby blanket of Iris's she never gave away. Here in Maine, she has started sleeping with it, clutching it.

"What a train wreck I've created," Pete says to himself, breathing in Alice's familiar smell and noticing that the look on her face is not one of contentment, but one of struggle, as if her mind were trying to work through something in the night that it couldn't quite arrive at the meaning of.

After years of being attuned to the smallest chirp from her girls, Alice awakens, even though Pete might swear he's not made a sound. "Pete," she calls out, her voice soft and wanting, any edge to it melted away in sleep. For a moment, his heart flutters with hope, a butterfly warming its wings in the first warm bands of morning light.

"Yes," he says, trying to sound steady, present.

"Are you coming to bed?"

"Yes."

Pete takes his pants off, his hat, his middleweight coat, then his fleece. For a moment the air feels good to him on his legs and through his thin T-shirt. He stands, letting goose bumps appear on his arms. He feels anticipatory, cautious.

"The moon is so bright up here," he offers. "I don't remember ever seeing it in the city like this, do you?"

"No," still-groggy Alice answers. "There is no moon in the city."

"Don't be ridiculous." He meant to sound funny. But it doesn't, he realizes immediately. He shouldn't bring attention to it. Maybe she took it as funny? Everything is a minefield.

Silence.

Alice has given him no sign that he is welcome in the bed right now, that they are okay, so Pete moves in his boxer shorts over to the low, broad window that looks out from their room across the white porch, then his eyes travel over the dark slate terrace with ghostlike white iron chairs strewn around in no particular order, and on down the field to the ocean and, finally, the horizon where ships sometimes sail at a distance. Their room is long and almost as wide as the entire house and they get both southern light and some east and west too. They are protected from the north in the wisdom of the old ship's captain who built this low cape into the hill, a man who knew the distance from the sea to his bed and the advantages of being near the ground.

As he looks out to the ocean, suddenly Pete has a memory: They'd taken the girls to visit some friends, Rob and Sandy, with a house on Martha's Vineyard. The friends were very connected, went to cocktail parties with the Obamas, lived in

Washington. That year he and Alice had contributed a large amount of money, and so had Pete's boss, and so they were all out there to go to a fancy fundraising party on the island and spend the rest of the weekend having beach picnics and drinking gin and tonics. "Those are two of the most elegant, beautiful people I've ever met," Alice said later over dinner, referring to Michelle and Barack. They'd all gone out to the Alchemy and ordered more drinks, lobster bisque, and rare bluefish. The next night, they did a beach picnic. The drinking started as soon as they had lifted the hampers of food out of Rob's Jeep. As the kids ran back and forth from the edges of the large, frothy waves, Rob pulled out the grill and started cooking up some turkey burgers for the kids, hamburger for the adults. There was a tension between Sandy and Rob that was hard not to notice, almost a chilly wind. Alice and Sandy were setting up the chairs and napkins and opening bags of chips and containers of sliced carrots, supplying towels to the damp children. As soon as the kids were all sitting down in beach chairs, the sand cleaned from their hands, sweatshirts pulled over goose-bumped chests, Sandy asked Rob to plate up their turkey burgers. She poked at one with a pink, manicured nail.

"Rob, these are raw," she said.

"No, they're not," he said, haughty sounding, the collar of his white Izod shirt imperious against his neck.

"You need to put them back on—this one is seeping bloody juice."

"Jesus, Sandy. I'm telling you they are fine. You worry too much."

"Get out of the way and I'll cook them." By this point she was standing right next to him at the grill, her Lilly Pulitzer dress glowing salmon in the sunset. Alice was standing with the children, handing around bowls of chips to tide them over and opening mini caffeine-free Cokes and Minute Maid apple juices. Pete was stuck standing next to the grill with Rob and Sandy, holding his drink with a perma-grin on his face, not sure how to move away without being obvious. And then Rob took his spatula and threw it in the sand, as if it were a plastic toy, and said, loudly enough for them all to hear, "You two," and he jerked his head toward Alice, "are cut from the same cloth." And then he stormed down the beach, drink in hand, his Nantucket-red shorts scrunching just a bit between his soft, pudding thighs.

Pete felt the color drain from his face. He realized his friend was insulting his wife. That their friends must not like his wife, or at least Rob didn't, and that Alice could be used as an insult. But instead of looking at Alice, instead of casting her a line, a sympathetic look, anything at all, he looked at Sandy, who, teeth gritted, was cooking the turkey burgers. And then he'd looked away. From both women. He'd aided no one.

Here in Maine, in this chilly room, waiting for his wife to speak, Pete thought about how he could have intervened somehow. And barring that, he could have made sure *she* knew he wasn't okay with the childish way Rob had acted. He, too, had punished her with his silence. Suddenly, as if getting boiled and sucked in by an undertow, it occurs to Pete that that was one of many times he could have been there for Alice, could have stayed connected, and didn't. The thought occurs to him: How many times can you abandon a person and have them forgive you?

Then, almost like divine intervention, Pete hears Alice say, "Pete."

Her voice is gentle, as if she didn't notice his earlier slight, or the thousands of slights before that one. "Do you ever think about what will happen to the moon with the planet and global warming and all that? Like, will it still guide the birds and oceans and fishes and everything?" she asks.

He answers, musing, almost to himself, as if he's ten again and lost in a textbook or one of the old *Scientific American*s his parents used to get. "I read once somewhere that the moonlight, when it's full, warms the earth a little. Or maybe that isn't right. Maybe it was something about how the earth is closer to the sun at a full moon. Anyway, the moon makes the tides higher, that much I know. And that will be part of it. Yes, with the rising seas."

"We are safe here, though. The ocean is way down that knoll." There's no question mark. It's better to affirm.

"Right."

"Are you done with your work?"

"Yes."

"I need to go to sleep. *Was* I asleep?"

"Yes. Sound asleep."

"Oh."

Silence.

Then, "Alice. I don't know how to say this exactly. But, since you are awake and it's quiet, and no one's here, I want to ask: Do you think you'll ever forgive me?"

Silence.

"Alice? Did you hear me?"

"Pete. I'm not sure I believe in forgiveness. Maybe one just endures. And then time blunts things. I don't know. I've been trying to figure that out."

A knife whistling through the cold air. Suddenly Pete isn't sure he can breathe.

And then he says, "You've always been my compass, Alice."

He hears her snort. Then, "You don't wear poeticism well, Pete."

He sucks in his breath and forges on. "Okay, maybe that's a stupid metaphor. But you tell me that 'I'm sorry' means nothing. I'm trying to use words that will mean something to you. I've been racking my brain to try to figure out how to say something I feel. I feel terrible; miserable. About so much. I feel almost crippled by what a shit I've been. I don't know how to communicate that." He can feel himself playing for her sympathy, a sob rising in his chest.

Her voice snaps like a whip. "But it wasn't enough. Being your *compass*, as you say. Maybe it *isn't* enough. I need to go to sleep, Pete. I am tired and sad and just . . . wrung out."

"Okay." He finds himself wondering if she knows that he betrays her nightly in his mind when he's outside, that he goes back into the thrill of the sex—only to come back to her, again and again. Is there a way to explain this? No. It would make it worse, he realizes. "I can't possibly express that correctly," he says out loud, not meaning to.

"What?"

"Nothing. I just can't seem to get to the right words."

"No. You can't."

After Alice falls back asleep, not moving, Pete lies awake, the moonlight making the white of the window casings seem so proper and tidy, like all is well in the world.

The next morning, Pete comes down after his family is awake. Groggily he pours coffee from the pot, his hair standing up off the top of his head, his face puffy. The weather has shifted and it's rainy and windy outside, the last blasts of March roaring around the house. Iris is playing with pink Legos and Sophie is reading a book. Alice is cleaning up from pancakes. There is a tepid-looking stack sitting on a plate that Pete assumes are for him, a pat of butter congealed on the top cake. A bottle of maple syrup sits next to them.

Pete clears his throat. "Hey, have you all seen the moon up here at night?"

"I have, Daddy," says Iris.

"Liar, you're asleep," says Sophie.

"No, sometimes I wake up."

"And waah waaah for Mama."

"Sophie, stop it," says Alice. There's that scary edge in her voice.

Pete clears his throat. Then, "I'll wake you up one night, girls. When it's really bright. It's unlike anything we've seen in the city."

"I love the moon," Alice says more to herself than to anyone. "I feel like it's my only friend."

"I'm your friend," says Pete, too unsure to make eye contact. He looks out the window at the barn, coffee cup in his hand.

She snorts again. When did she start snorting? "No, you're not."

"Oh," he says. He sounds wounded. He knows he shouldn't, since she is justified. And yet he can't help himself but play this one.

"Nice one, Alice," says Sophie.

"Sophie. You are safe. Marriage is its own island. With its own rules and regulations. Daddy is okay."

"Whatever, I don't care." Sophie gets up and stomps up the stairs and slams her door.

Pete sighs and picks up his plate of pancakes and pours the syrup on them.

From the corner Iris says, "I'll be able to hear you if you start fighting."

"Nobody's fighting, sweetie," says Pete.

# 4

### • • •

# Zoom

Behind Sam, I can see a painting of a lizard walking across a pencil. The pencil is finely sharpened, the standard Ticonderoga No. 2 color—mustard yellow. It has a pink eraser. The lizard's tail wraps around the eraser and its tongue shoots out beyond the pencil; there are letters floating in a night sky, like stars, and the lizard is pulling them toward its mouth with its tongue. The letters spell the words *perchance to dream*. In one corner is a small sliver of a yellow moon, the light glinting off the lizard on the pencil. I think it's a clever painting, if not exactly high art. Beats the stupid backgrounds some people have started creating on this bizarre platform that has become the way we communicate now.

I'm the only one in the Zoom meeting so far. Sam and I try

to make small talk about the world going haywire. My father is usually the first one on, but tonight he is late. Sam busies herself with something on her desk.

The prompt this week was "Describe a lie you've told." When it first came into my inbox on Sunday morning, I was blearily scooping maple yogurt into bowls for Iris and Sophie while reading "The Morning Newsletter" in the *Times*. My first thought was, Pete's the one who should do this. For a moment standing there, I felt like I was plunged into darkness thinking about my marriage and our troubles and how I feel like I will never get out of this worse-than-torpor situation we're in where we discuss nothing and nothing gets solved and yet here we are stuck together even though sometimes I want to stab Pete in his sleep. Around the edges of the actual crazy violence I feel is the deep sadness that my life just hasn't turned out like I pictured, despite the beautiful house, despite the beautiful children. I feel like I am stuck in that Talking Heads song: "And you may ask yourself, *well*, how did I get here?" David Byrne's voice zigzags through my head like some sort of annoying conscience and all the things that might have been (but aren't) conspire and line up into a stupid list of regret bullet points marching through my head on a long piece of 11" x 17" legal-size paper. *Seems* becomes *is* and *is* becomes *seems* and I feel like Hamlet, unable to move beyond supreme stuckness.

I can say that when I daydream, when I'm out in the garden, when I have a second to forget the cloud of shock and awe I feel about my life, my blown-up marriage, and the world right now, I feel this deep yen to be back in theater. I miss the collaboration, the voices, the way I used to rewrite on the fly as the actors physicalized my words. I loved the dark room, the lights, hearing the director's voice find meaning in sentences I'm not sure I even knew there was meaning to as I wrote. I loved the way music became so ethereal and moving in that space. Did I let it go too easily? Is that what that was? Another bullet point.

But this morning, as I spooned out the yogurt, my children became blurry and I gazed out beyond them to the hydrangeas leafing out around the front porch, punctuating the edges of the gray slate terrace with emerald green, and beyond that, to the darker blue-black ocean. It was one of those perfect May mornings in Maine: everything was green and smelled like wet dirt and lilacs and apple blossoms. Except for the assignment, which was threatening, like a thundercloud, to ruin it all. You're going to ask me to open my heart and tell you something? We're only on class number three!

I took the phone and went outside and navigated to WhatsApp. On the side of the house an azalea we've never been here to see bloom before has turned an outrageous pink. Iris calls it the cotton candy tree. It literally vibrates with bees making a rumble so loud that you might think it was traffic.

"Hello," Sadie answered. It was afternoon in England already. Sadie and her husband, John, were Americans, but moved to England to put their daughter in an English secondary school and have an adventure. They were both computer programmers and could work from anywhere. Then Brexit went into effect and then came the virus. Somehow in the middle of lockdown they began to sound semi-English, almost Canadian, and bought a new house and moved and were all just fine. Sadie had already been up for hours, cleaning her cat boxes, walking her dog, starting sourdough, making a blackberry pie. All the things Sadie has already done when I'm just starting my morning always make me feel better, like there's still hope for my own day.

"Hi. It's me."

"How *are* you doing?"

"Unsure. The house is a mess; like actual piles of cat hair and just . . . it's dirt in corners; everything is grimy, especially the bathrooms. I just can't get to it. It feels unendurable. It's hard to feel happy."

"For everyone."

"And the writing teacher, Sam, sent us a prompt about describing a lie you've told. All I can think about is all the lies Pete has told me. I can't even remember if I've ever told a lie. Not a big one. Or if I did, I don't feel anything about it anymore because all the lies he's told have obscured any memory of any lies I've ever told. Do you see what I mean?"

"You've told a lie, Alice."

"I am aware. I must have. But honestly, Sadie, I'm not shitting you. I can't think of one. I'm, like, blank. And then there's my dad in the class and I can't turn this around and write about Pete's lies. I have to find something that I can write about with my dad there, *listening*."

"Yeah. That's a pickle. Can you make it up?"

"I don't know. I think the class is supposed to be memoir. In other words, real!"

"I wonder what your dad will write."

"I have no idea why I suggested we do this together."

"For connection."

"It was a stupid idea. I should have just done the class myself. Pete says he's mowing the lawn today. There are so many dandelions. The bees are all over them. 'The ticks,' he says. The ticks are fucking awful. We also have either pantry or wool moths flying all about. How many plagues can we manage at once? I found a tick between Iris's toes the other night. Dog tick. But still. So gross. It was peeking its disgusting little head out."

"Not to change the subject, but the strawberries are a week or so early this year and I made this strawberry trifle last night and we literally ate The. Entire. Thing." Sadie has this way of emphasizing her exuberance with the placement of periods in the middle of her sentences.

"What's trifle?"

"It's layers of cream and strawberries, basically. Like shortcake, only with cubes of angel food cake. In a bowl. It's terribly English. I put a photo on Instagram this morning."

"Does it get all mushy?"

"I think it goes sort of soggy. But we ate it all, so we didn't even try putting it in the fridge. When do you have to write your lie thing by?"

"Wednesday."

"You have time."

"God, here come my kids. They're fighting. Already! The day hasn't even begun. And there's Pete now, thinking he's mowing the lawn—the man and his machine, dun-da-dun! I have to go. Iris, you put that rock down! Sorry. I have to go. Bye."

"Okay. Bye."

How had I gotten into this class anyway? It was Lois who had suggested the idea during one of our sessions out in the field, over that therapist version of FaceTime, Doxy whatever. Lois told me that now that we had the internet, I should poke around. That I should find a way to get back to writing on a schedule, that she felt I needed an outlet during this intense time of exhausting free fall, that I might need "a place to put down," Lois said, my "anger and resentment of Pete." A place to examine my vacillations between "zero empathy and an overabundance of empathy." A place to "write regret." "Also," Lois added, "it's time for you to figure out if you're still a writer." I hated Lois when she suggested it. Of course I'm still a writer, even if it's only in my head.

But later that night, I looked at a website I'd read about in *The New Yorker* called HireArtists.org and found a picture of Sam. Sam was pretty, with long brown hair that she swirled up on her head like Princess Leia, and in the picture she was wearing a cozy flannel shirt and that lizard painting was behind her. Her bio said she'd written three books, all memoiry nonfiction-type stuff, none of which I had ever heard of. But let's face it, I have been intensively parenting for the past eleven and a half years and it seems I have been living under a rock. Two of Sam's books were published by Yale University Press, and the most recent was published by Norton. That all seemed good, enviable.

It turned out she was starting a new writing class a week later. Impulsively, I joined. It was only three hundred dollars for eight weeks and included a weekly prompt and a Zoom class. It was on Wednesday nights at eight, after the kids were already in bed. Pete was always on the computer now, even at night, working on the "crisis." In his case, he didn't mean the health crisis, though of course that's what precipitated the crisis he was talking about. Or the race crisis. The one he talked about was the "global economic downturn."

I landed upon an idea early Tuesday morning. Pete and I had just been talking about the news, what had happened to George Floyd. The kids were upstairs on the iPad watching something on Curiosity Stream about termites. For a moment, as we stood holding our coffee cups in shock and upset as we discussed what had happened, Pete had raised his voice and I had started crying in my outrage and shouted, "This happened in my home city! Our country. It keeps happening. Goddammit. Who are we, Pete? *Who are we?* I want to leave."

"Where do you want to go now?" he asked, the tiniest hint of sarcasm in his voice. I had already made us come to Maine. What was next? Manitoba?

"Anywhere. I am not an American anymore." The truth of that felt like an enormous weight, a total shock to my nervous system. But somehow true too.

Iris came down just at that moment and stopped. She walked over and punched Pete in the stomach. "You're being mean to Mommy," she said and ran out the door.

"Wait," I called after her, tears slick on my cheeks, hoping to save Iris from her own turmoil, to explain what she had heard in a way that she could digest. But Sophie was suddenly in the kitchen. "We heard you fighting, you big jerks," she said. Pete said, "Mommy and I weren't fighting, sweetie. We were talking about the news." When I went outside after Iris, I could hear Pete explaining what had happened to George Floyd as best he could without terrifying Sophie.

When I was looking for Iris I was thinking about my childhood in Minneapolis, Floyd's city, and then I was remembering the time I tricked my little brother, Brian, into trying one of Dad's cigarettes. It's a story my dad already knows, so it's not a big risk. I guess it isn't so much of a lie, really, but a trick. Aren't they almost the same thing? I would write about that, I decided.

All my life, my dad had had a small podiatry practice not far from our home, and our mother worked the reception desk. I still remember Thursday afternoons as my favorite day of the week because my dad had had a free clinic, and people from all over Minneapolis came then, people of all different races and ethnicities. That's where all his most interesting stories came from: the kids and their parents, the people who lived in the neighborhood Section 8 housing, the vets. There were people who were flat-footed or had corns or gout that made them hobble, or gross green funguses that ate their toenails from within or childhood diabetes that made their feet go numb. At the dinner table, Dad and Mom would tell me and Brian all about the people—what they looked like, talked like—and all their afflictions.

They came home with boxed pizza and let Brian and me stay up later than usual, listening. Oh, I loved those stories! I can still smell the greasy boxed pepper-and-pepperoni pizza with the squishy crust and the smell of my father's beer on his breath, and then, after he was done eating, the cigarette he enjoyed while my brother and I had chocolate ice cream. In my twenties, I fantasized about writing a series of essays, or a play, about those nights, about how solid and safe they had felt and how the stories just seemed to unfurl with Dad's smoke into the air. For a while, I began sketching out scenes in a notebook. Then I shoved the notebook into that vinyl bin under the bed and I've never gone back. Another regret on the list.

What my dad might write is almost more preoccupying to me than what I could come up with. What lies has *he* told? Thinking about what they might have been seizes me with worry. Our lives growing up were so outrageously uneventful except for one year, when something happened, and my father lived somewhere else for a time. That strange year is still murky in my memory. It comes back to me in the oddest moments, like when I'm trying to go to sleep or when Pete is away on a trip, or when I'm bathing Iris. I have this one clear memory of that year: I was being dropped off by a friend's mother after softball practice and my dad was in the driveway packing his car with brown paper bags and cardboard boxes. And then soon after, I remembered visiting him with Brian in a little apartment near his podiatry office. We all sat at a small, square table, and our father had bought brownies, which he took out of a brown paper bag, each wrapped in its own little gray wax paper, and he gave us each a tall glass of cold milk. The whole apartment was brown; brown walls, brown couch, and a tan bedspread I had never seen before. And hanging out of the dresser was the pink loop of an arm strap of a bra. I remember that. Like the girl in red in *Schindler's List*—just indelible, all these years later.

When my therapist, Lois, asks me to go back to that time and plumb what comes up, I can only name it one way: "Scared."

"Of what?" asks Lois.

"I don't know. My mother never talked. About any of it. She was so strange and quiet—her mouth like a line in a cartoon. In the car, when she drove us anywhere, she was preoccupied. I remember the *flip flap flip flap* of the windshield wipers was the only sound in the car and her tension was so loud, deafening actually.

"I was scared of not being a family anymore. Of that bra strap. Scared of that, for sure. And of having to go back and forth, packing that bag every Friday before school. I hated that. It took me forever. I always made us late for school on Friday mornings. Brian was always so good about it. But I hated it, dragged it out, made it miserable."

"But then you were reunited. Your family was. So it's a lesson in love."

"I guess. I don't know, honestly. Was it? My mother changed. The whole thing changed. We were all back under the same roof, but . . . I mean, I'm living this now. I can't even believe that." And then my voice catches, like on a jagged piece of shale. My throat hurts and I'm fighting back tears.

"Sometimes it is right to stay for the children."

"I remember only what was lost."

When I sat down finally to write the story about the cigarette, it came out fast. I found myself realizing that my brother was only Iris's age, and how confused he was; he was so little, it occurred to me. Sophie generally considers her sister's arrival, and then lack of departure from her life, an enormous and irritating inconvenience. And I realized as I was writing that I felt the same way about my brother. I had forgotten that. I always felt so guilty about feeling that way that I tried to make myself believe I didn't. But then when I wrote about tricking him—finding Dad's pack on a shelf, snatching the matches, taking him outside, telling him it would be fun and taste good, like mint, because they were flavored Newport menthols—I had this empathy for Brian I hadn't anticipated. I was remembering his brown eyes, and how small his hands were holding the cigarette; how his little mouth puckered around it and how even though he looked wary, he trusted me. That was the part that killed me. He trusted me implicitly, as if it were a no-brainer. Now I get it: I was his big sister. Now that I've got a daughter who is a big sister, I realize how important that job is. How had I not known it back then? Why hadn't anyone told me? Or had they?

I forget if I was punished. I just remember that my brother coughed and coughed and my mother came around the corner and found us hiding in the hedges that separated our lawn from the neighbor's and how really fucking angry she was. "Your brother has asthma, Alice! How could you!" And then she picked up Brian and ran him, slung over her shoulder, into the kitchen to find his inhaler and to give him water and brush his teeth and get him to calm down from the coughing that had, by then, turned into crying and then wailing.

"I think I had to spend the rest of the day in my room," I wrote. "That's my guess. My parents never did anything more severe than that. But whatever the punishment was, it was nothing compared to the guilt I felt for scaring my brother like that, for scaring my mother. We didn't know all we know now about cigarettes back then. Or if we did, my parents didn't do anything about it; cigarettes were a part of our world. When my dad finally quit, I must have been in the eighth grade. Seems so long ago, now."

* * *

While Sam and I waited for my dad and the other students to come onto Zoom, I was watching her organize the papers on her desk and check her email, and I was trying not to look at myself in the little Zoom box, which is impossible to avoid, so I was obviously looking at myself. I could see gray in the part of my hair; it almost looked blond on the screen, but not quite, not enough to fool any millennial. Of course it was gray. Only a deluded getting-older person would try to see it as blond. There are permanent puffy sacks under my eyes, which, when added to the gray, are starting to make me look positively ancient. It's so odd, this process of getting older and watching my parents get older. I still remember myself and my thoughts at five years old. I remember talking in a whole other language I made up for myself. I remember squeezing into that little hiding place in the hedge; I can still smell the green woody smell of the boxwood leaves and the dirt soft under my bare feet.

When Sam wasn't looking, I experimented with angling my face different ways to look better and found that if I looked up at the camera, with my chin slightly lifted, then the sacks sank out of view and my eyes looked big and bluer, if that's even a thing. I would need to remember that.

Earlier in the day, Iris and Sophie had Zoomed with my dad. Obviously I don't think either one of them thinks about how they look on it, the novelty of it has blown their minds. A year ago this was not a thing. Now it's *the* thing. They took the iPad into the tent that Pete had set up in the yard as a diversion; the promise had been that we would sleep in it one night together. I had read a report in the *New York Times* by some well-meaning soul that yard camping would feel like a pause in the monotony of quarantine.

At one point, I looked out and saw that both Iris and Sophie had left the tent and my dad was likely still on the iPad, by himself, in the tent, talking to no one, and staring at the green nylon roof. I was sure he was waiting patiently. But still. Why would they do that? I went out onto the porch and yelled, "Sophie?! Is Granddad still on the iPad?"

"Yes, Mom. I needed an extension cord. I've got this."

"Where's Iris? Couldn't she stay with him?"

"How would I know where Iris is? Iris is cuckoo."

"Sophie, you don't just leave someone on Zoom in a tent!"

"Not my fault. It's Iris who left. You don't understand anything."

"Well, I do understand that Granddad is sitting in the tent by himself on Zoom. Did anyone tell him what you were doing?"

"Alice, you're stupid. And you don't understand. And I hate you. Goodbye." God, I can't stand it when Sophie calls me Alice.

Sophie glared at me for a moment longer and then zipped herself back into the tent. I could hear her restarting the conversation with my dad. Oh, his patience!

Now, where was Iris? "Iris, where are you?"

Iris reappeared from under a rosebush at the edge of the yard, her leggings dirty at the knees. In one hand was her plastic Black Beauty horse and in the other was a green plastic dragon.

"Iris, you can't just leave Granddad alone on Zoom in a tent. He's trying to make time to talk to you."

"I got bored, Mommy. All he wants to do is blah-blah-blah."

I understand. He does like to blah-blah a lot. It's tiresome. He's forgotten, if he ever did know, how to be with a small imaginative child. Maybe the expectations were just different in the seventies.

"Okay, go play. Come inside when you need a snack." And Iris was gone, back under the rosebush.

Since his heart attack a year ago, my dad is subdued, slower moving. He spells things wrong in his emails; easy things like *blueberries* have a *y* instead of the necessary *ie*, or *celebrate* has an *s* instead of a *c*. It honestly drives me crazy. He's supposed to know things. That's the natural order.

These days, with Covid, he's too vulnerable to even go out and get the mail. My mother goes in a mask to the mailbox with a bottle of bleach spray and wipes the mail all down on the front steps. He reads a lot. They watch shows on PBS. And now he has the writing class with me to look forward to each week.

Later, waiting for the class to start, it occurred to me that maybe, hopefully, it was soothing for my dad to be on Zoom alone in the green balloon of the tent for a little while. Maybe it was quiet. Easy. And then I was suddenly imagining what would happen if I left Pete and went home to my parents. Would they take me right now with Covid? Would I go alone? Would I take my kids, à la Nora Ephron in *Heartburn*? Obviously I'd have to take the children. This is the spiral. I go into it about a hundred times a day. And I feel terrible every single time. Shaking my head, I looked around and tried to focus on something, anything. There was Sam still busy on her screen. And there was a small ant on my desk that had scavenged a crumb, likely from my toast that morning, eaten hurriedly while I checked my email. The ant was tiny, the piece of toast enormous, by comparison. It was heaving the crumb up over its head. "Where are you taking that?" I asked it.

"I'm sorry?" said Sam, looking up.

"Oh, nothing," I said. "It was an ant." It was too hard to explain. Sam wasn't listening anyway.

"Oops! Your dad and Justin and Tami are waiting. Stand by while I admit them."

I saw my father first, before he saw me. He looked pixelated in the camera. He was in his little den at the front of their house, books stacked and then piled on top of the stacks on the shelves behind him. His hair was grayish white and stood up a bit from the top of his head. His beard was trimmed neatly and his eyes looked especially blue today. I saw him see himself in the camera and then reach up his hand to smooth his hair in the front. "Hi, Charlie," beamed Sam, looking up from her work and taking a sip of tea from a yellow mug.

"Hi, Dad."

My dad waved at me and said, "Hello, Sam and Alice." A moment later the third writing student, Justin, a black-haired, fortyish man, with a constant stubble beard and glasses, came on the call, and then Tami came on. Tami had blond curly hair and blue eyes.

Sam began the class by asking everyone how their writing life was. Did they carry notebooks this week? Did they find themselves writing more than just the prompt? We all did our best to answer the questions, but you could tell that we were all four poised, like waiting Slinkies, to read our prompts and get it over with. My dad always wanted to go first, his neediness so palpable. This was mostly fine with me, though I somehow cringed even more with hearing my father's writing than with my own. Something about how much he wanted attention and acclamation. A little boy in the front row of class.

But this time, Justin spoke up first. He said he needed to get it over with. Then he read a story about when he was six and he and his parents were in Italy. In it, his father told him to lie to his mother about where they had been when he and his dad were supposed to be out gathering food for dinner. The mother had asked for bread and cheese, tomatoes and olives, and something sweet, for after. (I liked hearing the food part; it lifted me from my worrying about reading for a moment. The food in Italy was so fresh and soft and easy to eat with unabashed gusto; Pete and I and the girls spent a whole month outside of Florence two summers ago. When I look back at that month, I wonder if we did anything more than just eat and eat and eat.)

But Justin and his father had gone to the bar on the piazza and come home with just some day-old *pane* and some cured olives for dinner—no tomatoes, no cheese, no cookies, no panettone. His father smelled like whiskey and the mints he crunched in order to cover up the whiskey smell. The mother was confused, Justin wrote. Then Justin wrote about coming out of his room that night to pee and finding the father drunk, sitting on a plastic chair in the shower, singing that Chuck Berry song "Johnny B. Goode," while the water pounded down on him.

When Justin was done, Sam extolled his writing enthusiastically. She said how "expertly," that was the word she used, he'd slipped into the child's viewpoint and how much it reminded her of the famous Roethke poem, "My Papa's Waltz."

Sam sat back from the camera and closed her eyes, pulling her knitted shawl on her chair around her shoulders. She was waiting for the next piece, for it to come "organically," as she said. The lizard's pink tongue shot out from behind her head. I knew I should offer to go next, save everyone from this purgatory. But Tami spoke up. "I'll read." Behind Tami was a framed poster of James Baldwin.

"With everything that's going on," Tami began, "I was remembering when I was five and starting kindergarten. This was Chicago, 1980. They had been working on desegregating Chicago public schools. And my mother decided she would drive me about fifteen minutes north to a white suburb to school. 'Girl like you needs a white education,' she told me. I had no idea what qualified me for a white school, but I do remember feeling special.

"I remember the first day. It was hot. I was wearing a dress my grandmother had made for me out of, I swear to God, some sort of Laura Ingalls Wilder–type calico. I think my grandmother thought white people wore those still in 1990, like it was 1890. And tights. Tights! My legs were burning up. Anyway, my mother walks me up the steps and takes me into the building. At the door to the classroom, she leans down and hugs me. She smelled like the eggs and bacon she'd cooked us for breakfast. I remember holding on to her. Suddenly it seemed like this school was so far away from her at the hospital where she worked and Grandma at home watching *Jeopardy!* and the soaps all day long.

"'Don't leave me here, Mama.'

"'You'll be fine. You'll see. You can handle this.'

"When she left, the whole world caved in for a second. I must have been crying. But then I felt this hand in mine. It was a white girl with blond hair named Megan. Her hand was soft.

"'Where are you from?' Megan asked.

"And I'll never forget this: I blurted out, 'I'm white!' Loud, so the whole class and teacher could hear. 'I'm white,' I said again. Like no one had just seen my mother hugging me. My mother who was the color of those brownies with cinnamon I liked to get from Mr. Phipps at the corner store, the ones with the crackly tops. My grandmother scolded my mother when she bought me one. 'Girl, those brownies not worth the fifty cents! They nothin' but some Duncan Hines mix with cinnamon and marshmallows and peanuts mixed in!'

"That was the lie I told. It was a lie that separated me from my mother and my grandmother. I knew better. Even if I could pass for white, I shouldn't have wanted to. I am still ashamed."

Sam was nodding. "Powerful work," she said. "You set that scene so well." Everyone else was quiet. We had to be careful; we were all white and no one wanted to say the wrong thing. I yearned to tell her that I understood, that even though I was white I knew what it was like to pretend you were something you were not. I wanted to tell her that my whole life felt borrowed, that I was never clear where I fit in or how. That I got what she did because it wasn't a Black thing to do, it was a human thing to do. And I was sure that even her grandmother would understand. But I said nothing. Everything that raced through my brain felt vacuous, insubstantial, maybe a minefield, all wrong. It was my father, Charlie, who spoke up then. "Thank you, Tami. You and I must have been on the same wavelength. Unsurprising, given what's happening."

Sam nodded vigorously again and then said, "Tami, thank you for your courage. Your piece really gets at the pain you must have felt in that moment and how confusing it must have been."

"If no one else is ready, I'll go now," my dad offered. He suddenly seemed more tentative than usual, which made me lean forward a bit to check him out on the small "gallery view" screen. Why is his voice shaking? I wanted to know.

He began: "George Floyd is dead. Protests began yesterday. Not far from where I live, shops are being looted and smashed. As I write this. Police are firing rubber bullets. Tear gas is being used. I can hear sirens outside my window and the television tells me the rest. I can't get out there and march even if I want to because it's dangerous. We have the virus, and then the police are dangerous, the looters are dangerous, whoever they are. I don't think they live here. People from here wouldn't do that. And all I can do is watch the television and listen out my window.

"You get to be my age, and you want it all to stop. It's like when your kids are fighting and all you need is the time to drink your coffee and read the morning paper in peace. There was a time, when my kids were little, when I might have gone out there and marched. Helped, somehow. Susan and I had a free clinic on Thursdays for people who were poor and needed help with their feet. I got to know some Blacks that way, people who came to the clinic. Other than that, our neighborhood was white and suburban. I play golf; always have. Went to Northwestern the whole way through. In medicine, in those days, even in Chicago, there weren't many Blacks coming up the ranks. Nor many women, for that matter.

"But I am an old guy now. And this is about lies. The lie I told was the one I told my kids."

Okay, I was sitting up straight now. I didn't want to watch my father but had to watch my father. What was he going to say? Was he going to talk about that strange year when he was gone and our mother stopped working and when he came back no one ever talked about what had happened? Was he going to choose now of all times to unburden himself? In front of these strangers? I felt my chest tightening and I wanted to snap the screen shut. What a terrible, desperate, stupid pandemic idea this asshole writing class was. I hated Sam with a passion all of a sudden.

"I told my kids it didn't matter what color you were, what

gender you were, that you can be anything in this country. And I told them I wasn't a racist. But I lied: I can tell you; I've felt fear when I am driving through an unfamiliar neighborhood and a Black man in a hoodie comes out. When a Black man cuts me off in traffic, I feel racism surface in me. I judged some of the parents who brought their kids to my clinic. I never judged the kids. I voted for Obama. And I agreed with him when he told young Black men to pull their pants up. I spent his whole presidency fearing he'd be assassinated. But what if he was just the symbol of something larger I should have been worrying about? Not his safety only but every Black man's safety?

"The culture is confusing, was confusing. It was like the messages I was given about how to feel about other people went against what was in my heart. I'm an old man now and I regret it. My father was an Episcopal minister. He and my mother taught me tolerance. But sometimes I was weak, not strong. And now, as this all swirls around my city, I am realizing that that racism inside me, those thoughts I had about Black men, about Black parents, those thoughts I never dealt with because I didn't have to, played a part, a bystander part, in this. I am guilty too. When I lied to my kids I lied to myself and I let things happen around me that shouldn't have. How do you carry a lifetime of regret? I wish my dad were here to ask."

He stopped reading and was silent. His face hung, tired. Was he about to cry? Jesus. This was a train wreck. I'm watching my dad miss his dad and he's my dad.

For a split second, selfishly, I'm relieved that's it, that he didn't go into that weird dark year when I was a kid that he's never really talked about or even apologized to me for. But that relief quickly morphs into worry. I'm not in charge, yet somehow I feel like I should say something. But that is Sam's job, and Sam is silent. What if Sam is mean to my dad? Or shames him? What if she kicks him out of the class? What if Tami gets angry or hurt or leaves the safety of the Zoom room? Would he have been safer in a Zoom room of four white people, or would white guilt make him less safe? Why did he write *that*? Suddenly, illogically, I was getting angry with my father for exposing himself and me too in this way. Couldn't he have written about a lie he told the manager of Home Depot? Like, "No, sir, I did not open this can of paint I'm trying to return even though it sure looks pried open."

Sam's eyes were still closed. Justin was shifting around, peering into the monitor through his glasses. He started to clear his throat, like he might be about to save my father, and then said nothing.

It occurred to me suddenly the burden Tami must feel to make the things white people said okay for white people. What did *that* feel like? Maybe it was like all the ways I had helped men feel okay about being fucking assholes to women; how many times at a party, in a job interview, or at a theater rehearsal had I bitten my tongue when a sexist joke or insulting innuendo was made? How often had I stood holding a drink at one of Pete's parents' cocktail parties in the summer and felt like I'd just been slapped by the comments of some mothball-breathed old geezer in a blue blazer who marveled at how "plucky" I was to "try to" write for the theater. The times I'd been shocked by the things husbands said about or even *to* their own wives, like the time I was picking Sophie up from a friend's and the husband arrived home just at the same moment and, taking one look at his wife, who was dressed up for their night out, remarked in front of all of us, "Are you actually wearing *that*?"

Now I'm wondering, should I even read my own piece, following my father's about how he was a closet racist? Thanks to me, he would now be revealed to also have smoked Newport cigarettes. (God, aren't those considered a Black thing?) And even worse, he was negligent enough to have left them around for me to foist on my brother when he was all of five.

Sam finally speaks carefully and says, "I think it's very brave of you to write what you did, Charlie. If you've read the book *White Fragility*, you will recognize that you've just reckoned with yourself and broken your silence. As a writer, you are working on your voice, who your character is—the character that is *you*—and you are trying to figure out how that voice will manifest itself. Phillip Lopate says that you should always try to say something provocative, something 'borderline dangerous' are his words. What makes your heart beat when you sit down to write it? What feels to *you* like *you're* writing something borderline dangerous?" She peered at us all in the Zoom room. It was a challenge.

Justin was free to speak. After all, Sam had just called his writing "expert." He could pontificate now from the seat of knowledge. "Charlie, I really liked how you threw in those details, like playing golf, and the kids in the clinic. It felt very real to me. Really raw." Justin leaned back, pleased.

Tami was still quiet. She didn't look angry, really. Just distant. I could see Sam's eyes flitting around on Zoom.

"Alice," came Sam's voice finally, "did you write something that's dangerous for you?"

"I tried," I lied. "But I couldn't write anything this week. My kids. I couldn't make the time. I'm sorry."

Sam looked back at me from the screen. She looked like she was about to say something, but it was my dad who spoke first. Ever the father, he stepped into the void once again. His voice was gentle. "That's okay, Pickle," he said, using his nickname for me, the same one I use for Iris. "Some weeks are better than others." I could tell he knew I was lying; likely protecting myself or protecting him or Pete or the girls. I'm guessing he thought it was his fault, for reading what he did, or for being in the class at all. I could see it in his face that he knew I'd shut down. He knew! But he covered for me anyway.

I could hear murmurs of assent from Justin and Sam about how sometimes the writing genie just doesn't visit. Tami nodded, the most animated she'd been for several minutes.

But I wasn't listening. I was overcome with sadness, like-I-might-weep-forever sadness, the sadness Sadie told me was mostly hormonal but I was never so sure if it was hormonal or just the-weight-of-every-bad-decision-I've-ever-made-in-my-life sadness.

Somewhere in that pea soup of longing and nostalgia for my dad, my childhood, guilt about my brother, and for my whole life that has passed by until this one moment in time where I could have written something brave but did not; this moment when I sat there silent while my father was the one who was courageous and vulnerable, I heard Sam say it was time to leave the meeting, that Zoom would kick us off soon. I hazarded a peek at my dad even though, by then, I could feel that horrible involuntary brimming-with-tears feeling I was trying so desperately to keep as pools instead of waterfalls until I could leave that horrible screen. He seemed okay. Tami looked okay. God, am I the only one who isn't okay?

"Good night, Alice," he said over the screen.

"Good night, everyone. Good night, Dad." Over and out.

I hit the red button to leave the meeting and went outside, gulping huge breaths of the lilac-scented air. Alone in the dark, I walked down to the water and stood by the waves and let myself finally cry about all of it: that crucial, unbearable "Mama" George Floyd had uttered at the end; the pandemic, my marriage, and The Fucking Her; my sweet children and how little they know and how much they know too. I cried about how long I have been carrying the mental load of our family with no time for myself. And, indeed, who *am I* now? I thought about my confusion about my father and my love for him too; how old he looked on the screen, how vulnerable; how I could've helped him tonight but didn't know how; how all I'd wanted during that class was to be free of him, to not have him hanging out in that Zoom room. I cried about my silence and how I could have made some gesture, said something that made Tami feel less alone, but I was too scared to say the wrong thing and that made me a coward. I cried about how when I'd tried to talk to Sophie about the protests and George Floyd, Sophie had said, "I don't want to know this stuff, Mom," and how, too harshly, I'd stupidly retorted, "Well, Sophie, if you were a twelve-year-old Black boy you'd have no choice," which made her look scared. I cried about that sudden painful feeling that seared through my breast that morning and made me feel ferociously that I didn't want to be an American anymore, that I could not tolerate another second of Trump and his cohort and the pain and inequality that was being inflicted despite everything I thought this country had stood for. I cried about how long I had been somnambulant; how it had taken George Floyd's life for me to finally wake up and get angry. Finally, I cried about the NPR news story I'd heard while making dinner. It was about Black Lives Matter protesters who had come out yesterday morning to clean up the mess in the street from the night's protests, and my heart had just broken when I thought about that kind of dignity—decency, really.

I was crying for a long time. I could feel cold snot running down my face and I was using the end of my shirt to wipe it off. I laughed at myself and thought of that owl in one of Iris's books who makes "tear-water tea" by thinking about everything sad in his life and the world. I'd practically made a pot of it myself out there. But still, I wasn't ready to go back inside. All that waited for me was bed. I'd sleep alone until two or three in the morning, when Pete finally came in from working late enough that he could watch markets open up around the world. By then, even if I wanted to talk to him, I wouldn't. Too many hours had passed alone. And where to begin, in which conversation?

I was shivering then and wondering how long I might cry for, would it never end? And then I heard something behind me and felt a warm hand on my shoulder and then Pete's voice.

"Hey. I didn't know where you were. Your dad called." Ugh, another twinge in my stomach. He always calls after the writing class. He likes to talk it through. I'd forgotten. Fresh tears burn my eyes.

"I brought you some wine." Pete hands me a glass of red and puts his arm around me. "You're cold. You okay?"

"No." I am angry and sad and I want him here and don't want him here.

And then Pete pulls me closer, and even though I'm not sure I want to, I find myself smoothing out the angles of my left shoulder and then softening into his chest. More tears come, more snot. "It's just all of it," I say.

"I understand" is what he says.

# 5

• • •

# Peonies

It's the peonies that remind me every June; their fat puffy heads that smell so heavenly, the ants crawling all over them, the way they give it up, petal by petal, until suddenly they are extravagant.

There's a woodchuck hole under the peonies on the north-west side of the barn, where those light pink, feminine blooms grow along the gray shingled, man-made structure. This year, there've been three baby woodchucks venturing out from under the barn, at first no bigger than croquet mallets. One of them is still so tiny that we've started calling it Runty.

Iris loves to sit at the big window in the dining room where there's a deep ledge that we use as a place to pile mail and put the fruit bowl. She shoves her little body in, inevitably knocking bills and stacks of who knows what onto the floor. She sits on her knees, looking out. Everything outside that window is magic to Iris; the chickadees and cardinals flitting about, Runty munching on tender grasses. Until we got here, I had no idea how hungry my children were for air and soil. What does Joan of Arc say in Shaw's play?

"To shut me from the light of the sky and the sight of the fields and flowers; to chain my feet so that I can never again ride with the soldiers nor climb the hills; to make me breathe foul damp darkness . . . without these things I cannot live."

On mornings like these, during this long stretch of an endless, misty spring while our lives hover in this borrowed and luxurious suspension, it is easy to forget the troubles of the world, or my own.

Anyway, the peonies, yes. There's that Jane Kenyon poem where she calls them "outrageous flowers." This year, seeing them bloom in Maine for the first time, my first June here, and taking the time to really watch them go from those tight little balls to these luxurious Victorian pom-poms, I have seen what she meant. And then, as if they know how overly—no, outrageously—blessed they are with good fortune, rather than hold their heads high with pride, they droop like little supplicants, heads down, apologizing.

Peonies are in June and it was June. A Sunday. Pete had taken me to meet his family in Westport. His parents, Joan and Richard, had gone to church that morning. Joan was wearing heels and had this way of walking like a cat, I noticed, all toes and her shoulders up and poised, her breasts out, a finishing school affectation from another era. We were all in the dining room, eating dinner. Chicken breasts with some sort of clear jus and asparagus, I remember that. Nice bone china and clinkety-clink silver. A silver vase of peonies on the sideboard.

Pete and I had been together almost three months by then. I spent almost every night at his place, and in the mornings, I took Finn out for walks in the park. Pete no longer needed his dog walker. In the afternoons, while he was working, I went to waitress and then came back to him late at night, when he was in bed, or just coming home from beers out with clients or friends. When I went to my apartment, it smelled stale and there was dust on my desk, on my notebooks, on the manuscript of the play I was working on. I kept thinking I'd come back for a week-end, or a week, and clean and then write, come back to myself and my own work, that this would all stop and I'd go back to my life. But somehow it wasn't happening. Time was hurtling along and I was, well, *ensnared* isn't the right word, as I wasn't struggling. I had just fallen into this new world that spun around Pete and his life, and it was terribly exciting and also, at the same time, left me with some kind of odd vertigo.

So, there we were eating in the early evening spring light in the dining room, sitting at that dark cherry table with that chicken and asparagus and drinking a lovely white wine that had the tiniest hint of fizz to it, and Pete raised his glass and said he had a toast to make. We all looked up, and he took my hand and he said, "Mother, Father, I want you to know I am going to marry Alice. She doesn't know it yet. She might not even say yes. But I know it. This is my future wife." And then he laughed and said, "Gotcha," to me and winked.

I almost dropped my glass—I think my heart stopped. It was terribly brazen and insanely sexy of him to do that, and also there was a dangerous feeling to it. The chips were now down in a way that would be hard to undo. His surety was the thing.

There was this odd and silent pause, and then Joan just said, "Oh. Okay. I see. We'll need to get the floors redone for an engagement party." And then sipped her wine and cut into a spear of asparagus with her fork. Richard Sr. smiled and then nodded absently at his wife to acknowledge the comment about the floors. He murmured congratulations to Pete and me, and Joan remembered to smile primly. My good God, where do they teach WASPS to be so detached?

There was a gentleness to Richard, though. He had a kind and tall boxlike face, his jaw very square and strong, his hair gray-going-white, and his eyes very blue. I liked him; there was something very quiet about him, very thoughtful, like he'd just stepped out of a Sargent painting and into the world and was still getting his bearings. He loved to read books and watch birds. You could find him more often than not standing in the dark, deep-blue-walled library with binoculars around his neck, looking out the window past the yard and into the thicket of alder and knotweed beyond, picking out warblers and sapsuckers.

Later, when the day was ending in that lovely gloaming light that is somewhere between dusk and darkness and the sky turns sapphire, Pete asked me to go out for a walk before bed. By then we'd had lemon meringue pie and coffee in little cups with pansies drawn in gold leaf on their creamy sides and sat with his parents and watched a documentary about the Royal Family and all that Diana business. Since dinner, my heart had been clanking in my chest and it was making me dizzy. When Pete touched my hand, I felt like I was on fire; when he spoke, my breath caught in my throat.

Outside on the gravel walk, in the heady smell of peonies, the sky all blue and the moonlight making everything silvery, Pete started to laugh, that big, all-encompassing laugh he has, and it made me laugh and suddenly I was running out across the clipped, green lawn until he caught up to me and grabbed me around the waist and kissed me.

"You realize," I said, "you need to actually do it?"

"Do what?" He laughed and kissed me on the nose, and then the forehead, and then, taking my hand, he got down on one knee and held my hands and looked so earnestly up into my face and said, "Will you?"

And then, "Wait—before you answer. I have this . . ." And he pulled out a little red leather box that was worn on the edges and fitted with a tiny golden clasp, and when he opened it, I saw that inside was a lovely, simple ring of gold with a circle of perfect gray pearls and what, I later learned, was a yellow diamond at the center; it looked almost more like a sea creature than a jewel, animate somehow. "This was my grandmother's," he said. "If I'd had a sister, it would have been hers. But my grandmother gave it to me. And I want you to know, Alice, I really hope you'll say yes—I—God, I've never done this before. Ha!

Obviously. I'm shaking. Alice, Alice, my fair Alice . . . Will. You. Marry. Me?"

And I said, "Yes." I said yes. Of course I did.

The engagement party was to take place in mid-sweltering-July in Joan and Richard's long, green backyard. Joanie had rented a tent. They had a large guest apartment that sat over a capacious and newly built garage, rec room, and small ceramics studio for Joanie. My parents would sleep there, with Brian and his girlfriend, Marianne. Pete and I would stay in the main house. By then, the floors would all be polished to a deep mahogany, overlaid here and there with thick oriental rugs.

The wedding itself would be my family's affair. I had chosen the Brooklyn Botanic Garden as my location, almost a year later, in May. When Pete told his mother that the wedding was going to be small, low-key, Joanie was confused. At least that's what Pete told me. His mother always envisioned large weddings for her boys with lots of friends and family. Joanie and Richard were big donors to the Democratic Party, the local YMCA, the Fresh Air Fund, Save the Children, and countless other places; for them a wedding was a chance to renew their connections. After all, Joanie went to Wellesley, "with Hillary," she always said.

For the engagement party weekend, Joanie went all out. She hired a catering company and had retained two employees, from six a.m. until eleven p.m., to serve muffins and coffee and make made-to-order omelets on Saturday morning and then quick chicken salad sandwiches or snacks and cocktails at a whim, because, "heavens knows, people get hungry at unpredictable times," she said. The official event, with all their friends and some of mine, would take place Saturday, late afternoon, outside. On Friday afternoon, both she and Richard stood outside the old house to welcome my family, like a scene from *Gosford Park*. They had hired a lanky kid—was he thirteen?—his name was Henry, a neighbor's son, to help all weekend. Henry took my family's bags up to their rooms and showed them that the fridge was stocked with mineral water, toast, butter, and eggs. Joan had thought to put fruit in a bowl and bags of chips and boxes of crackers in the cupboard.

On the day of the actual event, lots of ladies in soft dresses paraded into the house and lots of men in blue blazers. Cocktails were handed round and round. I stood with Pete at the door in a light pink dress and smiled and said hello as Richard and Joan introduced me. The whole affair was bigger than my wedding ended up being; people fanned out onto the lawn and Richard made a toast to Pete and me and everyone murmured some sort of "Hear, hear" and raised their glasses and gold bracelets slid down wrists and gleamed in the sunlight. Then the party slowed down and some guests moved inside for warm hors d'oeuvres, and I was able to sit down with a cup of coffee.

In the corner of the living room was a large lemon tree with polished leaves—I swear to God Joanie must have paid someone to dust that thing—and I found myself sitting on a low bench near it, watching and listening. I wasn't hiding exactly. Just taking it all in. There was conversation about the country club and the war and the economy. There was Joan bustling in and out. Where was Dickie, Pete's brother? I don't remember seeing him in the living room. He was there; he must have been.

Pete once told me that when they were little he and Dickie would play hide-and-seek. As the game evolved, it became a game about staying hidden the longest, and waiting until their parents freaked and then figured it out. Pete told me that sometimes it would take hours; their parents had no idea they were even gone, nothing signifying that the house was quieter than usual. I looked at him skeptically when he told me that. By then we had two children and *quiet* was not one of the words I would use to describe anything my girls did.

"No," Pete convinced me. "With us, it was all about hiding. We were masters at it. Dickie perfected it and I learned from him—the weird gully behind the forsythia; the chest of photos in the attic—I can still feel those photos sticking to my bare knees and cheeks, and the dusty smell inside that hot chest; once I even put on a pair of my mother's heels and stood inside one of her dresses in her closet for, God, it must have been hours, me breathing in her Chanel No. 5 and that soft feeling of silk on my body."

"Did you ever get in trouble?"

"Once, when my father was home. He spanked me. Hard. My mother was very upset and she had made him angry with how upset she was. I think that was the time I'd gone down the road a bit too far . . . I was hiding behind the neighbor's bulkhead. I remember the concrete and some daffodils back there."

"Did you do it again?"

"Oh, sure. Dickie loved to do it. He always appeared before I did, though. It was like a test. I was better at it; I liked the danger of it. But I got in more trouble than he did."

After all those guests left there was the dinner with my family and his, in the dining room with the silver service and buffet and the caterers still waiting on us. The dinner was long, and by the end I was tired and just ready to go up to Pete's old room to fall into his bed with my new copy of *Harry Potter and the Half-Blood Prince*.

But I knew there would be after-dinner chat and then more coffee and then saying good night. While I counted the minutes, whiskey was poured for a nightcap.

Eventually, my parents went out to sleep across the driveway and Pete opened his laptop. The caterers were cleaning up our mess, and without anything else to do, I helped them stack plates and bring them into the kitchen. On one of the trips carrying plates, I heard Joan in the library. I saw the door was open and Richard was sitting at his desk. Joan was standing by the window looking out into the darkness. Both held glasses of whiskey, and Joan said, "Do you think she'll hold his attention?"

"Why do you ask, Joanie?"

"She is rather plain. Well, not plain exactly; she has all the raw materials—beautiful hair, nice eyes, nice figure. But she presents in a common kind of way, don't you think? All those jeans and T-shirts and never so much as a smear of lip gloss."

"I like to think Petey is growing up. Concentrating on what matters, not all that razzle-dazzle."

"I wonder."

"Her parents seem friendly."

"Very Midwestern, aren't they?"

"Yes. The mother is a bit skittish. But the father is solid."

"I just hope he knows he wants this. He was always such a changeable child."

"Petey?"

"Yes, dear, Peter. Who else are we talking about?"

"Humph. He knows when to buckle down, get the job done."

"Did you?"

"What do you mean?"

"Buckle down?"

"Of course I did. I'm here now. Please don't bring that all back up, Joanie."

"No. No point."

And then it was quiet. I heard Richard clear his throat and say, "I am going to go up," and his chair shoved back and I realized I was still holding a stack of plates and standing there like a lemon. I handed the dishes off in the kitchen and found Pete in the living room staring at his computer. "I need to go to bed," I told him.

"I'll be right up," he said, he's always said. Hours later, I was lying in the dark as he slipped into the bed next to me.

"What took you so long?"

"Dad and I were watching the end of the Yankees game."

"Oh. I thought your father was going to bed."

"No? My mother went to bed."

"Did the Yankees win?"

"Yes. Seventeen to five."

"Are your parents okay with all this?"

"Of course. Why wouldn't they be? They love you."

"I see."

"Babe, I'm about to pass out."

"Good night."

When Pete and I first met, I was different. I used to pull my hair back tight. I was partial to jeans and T-shirts and sneakers. When I was writing, I wore a baseball cap. Soon Pete changed all that. He encouraged me to let my hair down; I added some blond highlights to it and started every so often to wear dresses and skirts. I shaved my legs more and got a bikini wax. I started to smooth out. I was happy to make those changes for him. At least I think I was happy. Even so, I could never quite shake the feeling that underneath the fancy hair and silk dresses, I was still a tomboy who liked to climb trees and ride my bike through puddles, who still wanted to roll in piles of wet leaves in the fall. I could never quite shake the notion that I was plain.

In that year between our engagement and our wedding, Pete was quickly rising at his firm, and I was working, on and off, in between planning the wedding, on a play. But it was hard and slow because I needed it to be the next better thing after the small success of the first. All along, I was waitressing at the French Roast café around the corner from us, on Broadway. There were these two sisters who came in often—at least every couple of days, to see each other. They both had long—down to their asses, long—brown hair that was perfectly brushed, and they had a similar style of big cashmere sweaters and tight jeans and lovely leather boots. They would smile when I came to their table; recognition was everything. Each time they ordered the same thing, every time: two cups of coffee and a pitcher of honey. I had never heard of honey in coffee. Once, they convinced me to try it. I did and thought it was terrible—cloying and tasting something like thinned molasses. I didn't say anything to them. At the end of my shifts at night, I ordered the same thing: a blue-cheese burger with onion and tomato, and I slathered ketchup and mayonnaise on it. No burger has ever tasted that good.

The restaurant was owned by an Israeli with a shaved head and a lined camo jacket. Some of the waitstaff and the manager were Israeli too; all of them had done their military time back home. Ari, the manager, wore square tinted sunglasses, even inside, and he was a lanky guy who liked to be silly and loved drugs and cigarettes. When the owner wasn't around, Ari could be found outside at one of the little café tables, drinking coffee and smoking, trying to revive himself from the partying his body had endured the night before.

In the kitchen was Jesus. No joke, that was really his name. He spoke English with a strong Mexican accent and uttered a long torrent of swears in Spanish if we chatted too long by the pickup window or when we forgot a side of mayo. My friend Eric liked to do a little dance just to irritate Jesus and sing loudly, to the tune of the *Pirates of Penzance*, "I am a tyrant king . . ." And then he'd pirouette and grab a BLT and off he'd go belting, "Dah dah dah dah dah," to the same *Pirates* tune.

After a while, Pete told me that I didn't need to waitress anymore; then he said that he didn't want me to, that it embarrassed him. Plus there were things he wanted to do in the evenings and my job was getting in the way. Eventually it was just easier not to waitress, and I decided to try harder to be a writer. We had merged our bank accounts, or rather Pete added me to his and I closed my checking and my minuscule savings, so I didn't need to worry about bringing money in. With the time that opened up, we went to dinners and parties and we saw plays on Broadway. When he was at work I felt increasingly marooned from the theater world I was writing for. I no longer felt like I could relax at my dusty and now-unfamiliar desk; writing in his apartment was strange; coffee shops didn't work. My world was slipping away, ever so slightly at first, and then before I knew it, it was just gone—vanished. I woke up one day in a life I didn't recognize. I didn't even recognize myself. But that took longer to realize.

* * *

Pete and I got married in the Brooklyn Botanic Garden on Sunday, May 6, under the cherry blossoms in the Japanese garden. No peonies yet in bloom. It was nine a.m. and still cool and damp, the clouds threatening rain. I wore black Hunter wellies under my dress until I got to just before the little bridge I was to walk over, where I switched to shiny, shimmery, mica-colored heels. Pete wore a gray suit that matched the clouds.

Pete had told me we could get married anywhere, his parents would pay for it. But I said no. I needed to be outside, rain or shine. "I need something lovely," I told him, and something my parents could easily take care of. I wouldn't give Joan the satisfaction of paying for our wedding.

I remember pulling those heels on and coming across that bridge under the blossoms.

The dress: I had gone home that spring to Minneapolis and my friend Betsy and I went to a few bridal shops around town until we ended up in one on Main Street and picked it out. I liked it; it was long and sheer and hugged my hips. To me it was understated and classy, simple in a way I approved of and I thought would accentuate my long hair and the flowers, the lushness of the blossoms around me.

After the ceremony, we walked over to Tom's Restaurant and had breakfast: waffles with whipped cream and strawberries, mimosas, bacon, fruit salad. We took over the whole place until about noon, when they opened back up for lunch. It was over before you knew it.

Pete and I took the subway home, me in my dress and holding my bouquet of lilacs and he in his suit, and people smiled at us and a man handed me a bouquet of pale pink roses he was bringing home with his groceries and said, "I cannot help it, you look so lovely. Congratulations." We walked the five blocks to our apartment, Pete's apartment, and took the elevator up, and I'll never forget this, but he helped me out of my shoes and my dress and brought me an old soft T-shirt of his and a pair of his boxers to put on and sat me down on the couch while he made me a cup of chamomile tea and a huge stack of buttered toast, cut into triangles. He took off his suit jacket and sat down next to me, a beer in his hand, and said, "Tell me everything about the day." And we talked until it was dark and then we ordered Chinese. It was the most romantic afternoon of my life.

# 6

● ● ●

# Solastalgia

It's gotten so hot here suddenly. And humid! Summer has tipped mercilessly into its fullest capacity, turning everything decadent and damp. A pumpkin Iris planted has leaves the size of elephant's ears; but like a huge octopus reaching out of a cage, it has taken off out of the garden and is traveling across the yard, recklessly reaching its tentacles hither and yon. Slugs and bugs abound outside and little ants case our indoor counters all day long; we do our best not to rinse them down the drain because I read once that their little armies actually help keep bad bugs out of the house. There's steam in the mornings that comes off the thick grass as the sun comes up, and the ocean is still and blue like it's waiting for us, patiently, silently, to come play.

Or, God, a shark is waiting. Holy hell, did you hear about

the woman swimming with her daughter a few hours south who died from that great white shark attack? In Maine? I saw the news at night, when I was in bed. I went downstairs to the office to find Pete and tell him.

"Too cold up here," Pete assures me. "Don't worry."

"How many things do we need to be terrified of?" I ask. "What comes next? Locusts? Rabid skunks? Russian drones? Will there be a shark hunt with fishermen all up and down the coast hunting it at night, their torches burning in their gnarled hands, their grizzled beards waxed with whale blubber?"

"I don't think they can do that," Pete tries, an incredulous smile breaking across his handsome face. He likes the role he gets to play in moments like these—the straight man to my hysteric. I like it too, and play my part to the hilt.

"I don't know what is allowed and not allowed anymore. We have Trump and the pandemic. QAnon, for fuck's sake. Oregon. Those no-mask-wearing buffoons. Black Lives Matter. The planet burning up. RBG in the hospital; she'll likely die before this election. People are outraged. Scared. *Everyone's scared*, Pete. Or they're just fucking angry."

"Alice, I think there's some general consensus that the shark issue is global warming and seal populations. I don't think anyone blames the sharks."

"Bullshit. Those militia people will blame the sharks."

"They are in Michigan . . . Landlocked, lakes . . . Anyway, I get your point . . ." He trails off and is typing and staring at his screen. "Look at this website—it's our local ABC News from the city. The comments are hilarious. Like this one from someone named Rascal: 'It appears that people from New York can't go anywhere without pissing off someone . . . or something.' Or this one, from Trevor: 'I love the sharks. The sharks are telling the people to stay home during the Covid pandemic.' Or this guy, Rusty: '100 percent of shark attacks happen in water, so stay out of water and problem solved.' This is my favorite: 'White sharks matter!' No, no, this one, from a guy named Harold: 'There was a two-hour PSA about this kind of thing in 1975. It was called *Jaws*.'

"Alice, seriously—most everyone on here—I'm looking right now—is saying what you're saying: warmer waters, sharks live in the ocean, overfishing. I don't think any of these mostly sane seeming people will agree we should all go out and kill sharks."

"I'm still worried."

"You're worried because everything is worrisome. It makes sense. It's a shit sandwich right now."

"Lovely analogy, Pete."

"I'm just sayin'. . . . I read this article, I don't know, last year, maybe, that something like two point five million sharks are killed every year for cosmetics. There's something in them—squalene, I remember that, it sounds like squaw—they use it for vaccines too. They'll need it for the Covid vaccine. Sharks may be on their way out—"

"Pete. I'm not joking. I can't take any more." These roles have suddenly gotten tiresome. I feel damp and exhausted. We know too much about each other now, sheltering in place this long. Like sometimes I don't know if I can bear one more second of Pete's loud and long waterfalls of pee into the toilet, his Pandemic Pees, as I've dubbed them. When he says he needs to go, Sophie says, "See you in twenty minutes," and then the girls and I all wait for thunder. Iris never flushes the toilet and Sophie leaves a tornado in the bathroom when she showers. When Pete farts, the smell seems to Velcro to the cloying, dense air.

Tonight, I move a pile of papers and plop down on the little striped couch in his office, defeated. "Right," he says. "No more shark facts." And then he smiles like the Cheshire Cat. "You look cute. I haven't seen you wear that Ryan Adams T-shirt in forever. Where was it?"

"Here. In a drawer. I thought twice about wearing it. Since he seems to be a creep."

"I remember when I got it. You suddenly look like you need a hug."

"Okay," I say. And as he stands up and comes to hug me, I feel my body go rigid as zings of hurt and anger compete with the soft, familiar feeling of his chest against mine. Will there come a moment when I am comforted again? He kisses my forehead and says, "Go get back in bed. I'll be up soon."

Our room is dark and there's this low, doomish thrum, like a tiny cello playing a sad melody just under the surface of absolutely everything and it's yanking at my heart. The other morning, I read an article on my phone in the *Time*s about polar bears going extinct. It was the picture: a bear standing on its hind legs at the end of an iceberg looking off into the distance. For what? Help? In a *New Yorker* from a few weeks ago, I read about the plastic masks and gloves from the pandemic getting in the oceans. Now sharks are coming north to eat seals but are eating mothers. And mothers, I fear, will be wanting them dead.

It's too much to bear in this heat, in this strange hovering place we're in. We are forever suspended in the unrelenting quotidian of life on pause. It is both strangely relaxing—a never-ending Saturday—while always being slightly uncomfortable because of its lack of structure or form; lack of places to go and things to do; lack of space and time away from our girls to fix anything between Pete and me. We have no friends here in Maine, no one to visit, even at a six-foot distance. Isolation was the point of this house—it was our own little island, while other New Yorkers with second homes here went to fundraisers at the Brooklin library and schmoozed over Brie on their wooden boats.

But us, we have no real connection here to anything but the blades of grass on our lawn, the rocks and little sandy spots between them on the shore, the trees and lilacs, garden and woodchucks. What was originally planned as fresh air now feels stifling.

At night in the damp heat, we are attacked not by sharks but by hordes of merciless teeny-tiny bugs that sting when they bite. They make me want to scream and cry, which makes Pete laugh until he wants to scream as well. For a week, or maybe it's been two, despite the bugs, and despite the heat that appears, thankfully, to have drugged Iris into a deeper sleep in her own bed, Pete and I fall sweatily into each other's bodies, with a feral intensity. The sex is so hot—our hands and mouths all over each other, exploring, giving and taking—that it's reminded me of our first days together. Lying in the air on top of our sheets, spent and catching our breath, the bugs find their way onto our softest, most private places to bite and bite and bite again.

"What the fuck are these things? I can't even see them!" Pete exclaims while slapping at his ankles. "Did we suddenly get bedbugs?"

When Dale came with his trailer and truck to finally moor our boat, the *Mrs. Dalloway*, the air was especially hot and the sun singed my arms. All night I had been bitten by the bugs. I had welts on my shoulders that I hadn't been able to stop scratching. These bites ooze after a while. When Dale hopped out to say hello, he looked at my shoulders and arms and said, saucily, "No-see-ums get ya?"

"No-whats?" I asked.

"The tiny bugs, come right through them screens. No-see-ums." He grinned a lascivious grin and stuck a cigarette between his lips.

"Is that what they are?" I asked. "My God, how come they never got us before—during other summers?"

"Ya got heah too late. They're a mid-late-July fee-nom 'round heah. Though, truth be tol' they're fee-ahss this summah."

Pete was laughing. "My God, Dale—Alice is about to go fucking crazy with those things. Last night she got into bed with bug spray all over her. She was like a citronella bomb. I couldn't breathe."

"Yeah, and he's hiding under the covers! Of course you can't breathe in there! You laugh at me, but you're just as freaked out by them."

"Nah," said Dale. "You just need fans—blow fans at yourself in bed and that'll blow 'em away."

When the boat was in the water finally, and Dale had left, I asked, "Isn't there anyone else? That asshole cut down our trees."

"We don't know if it was him," said Pete.

"Well, he told someone."

"Maybe. Or they just saw our car. Anyway, he was only protecting his own. I respect that."

"From us, Pete."

"I don't know who else to call. It's too complicated for me to figure that out these days. Let it go. He's competent at what he does for us."

In truth, the *Mrs. Dalloway*, with her loud motor and blue canvas cabin, is our ticket away from the house. Yes, we bring ourselves. But even with ourselves coming along, Pete gets the boat ripping over the water and the air in our hair, and when we finally stop at a little island beach and get out to swim and look for crabs, the tedium of our lives is cracked open, just the tiniest bit. We come home, salt sprayed and happy, almost as refreshed as if we'd gone to the Bahamas.

In this heat, when we aren't having sex, Pete and I have been fighting more than ever. I am enraged about The Her. The more sex we have, the angrier I am about it when morning comes. How could he have jeopardized all this? How come he never told me he was ready to step out? How come he just couldn't wait until we had more time?

He has no answers for me. And I don't know what to do about my fury with us all marooned here together, with the problem of still loving him, even so. One night I drove out into the dark at one in the morning, telling him I was leaving him, "for real this time," I said. I drove around in the dark with the windows down until I finally drove back home. He was in Iris's bed, sleeping with her, when I came in. His lack of worry that I might not come back felt like a sucker punch. Alone, I went to our bed and lay awake until sunrise. The next morning we didn't speak to each other. That night our sex was more passionate and sustained than ever. At the end, tired and still angry, I cried. Pete said, "Don't cry. I feel so connected to you right now."

All day, the girls run in and out, out and in, the screen door driving me crazy with its "Screech, bam! Screech, bam!"

"Stay outside," I shout. "I will be right there!"

No matter how late we are awake lovemaking, Pete gets up at dawn to check the closing Hong Kong market. He watches the news, and when I wake up he tosses me little savory bits: Trump referring erroneously to the "1917 Pandemic." ("Good God," says Pete. "The total fucking moron. The movie was called *1917*. The flu was in 1918!") And, "Portland is still nuts. Someone caused a fire in a courthouse. But Kate Brown still rocks and federal troops have to stand back." And, "The French are blaming a Covid surge on 'the irresponsibility of young people.'"

The girls and I sleep late, starting our days with a rush of adrenaline; the sun has already been up for hours. Iris wakes up and says, "What have I missed?" Sophie opens her eyes and snarls at the hot, relentless sun. If she sees Pete, she hurls a nasty comment at him about always being on his "device"—that's the word she uses now. It is such a grown-up-sounding word. And it sounds so much like *vice*, which, I guess, is not lost on her. Her simmering anger at Pete is inherited from me. I know that. Serves him right, I think. It's wrong of me to think that way. But I can't stop. I almost like it, or need it, sometimes. And then I feel guilty.

In the heat, the girls and I have been braving the "no-see-ums," and now, also, mosquitoes, to go out and dig potatoes, examine the tomatoes, tie up the bean plants, shade the romaine when it sags in the sun, pull a stray weed or two, and pick off a cabbage worm we have spent a good twenty minutes looking for while slapping at the bugs that are biting our ankles and wrists. When we spot the fleshy, repulsive green body of a cabbage worm, we grab it and mash it on the ground with a rock until its green guts snap out. There is something so satisfying about killing something small and gooey and for which I have no remorse.

What the girls and I have put together is not a big garden—just a few rows in an old rotting raised bed that has been covered with weeds ever since we bought the house. But it's something to watch and hope for, and it passes the time while I single parent and Pete works and works and works away inside. We marvel as the little peas climb up the strings we tied to sticks to make a trellis.

One evening, I asked Pete to help me prune the tomatoes like I'd read to do in the *Times*. An hour later, after leaving him to his own devices with clippers, I find him standing triumphantly next to our three plants, which have been all but denuded, the fruit hanging like bare testicles, all foliage shaved off their shafts.

"Wow, Pete. You read *Men's Health* on your phone this morning and get insecure or something?"

"What?" he asks, his smile dissipating. I just look at him, waiting for him to get it.

"Shut up," he says. "I was trying to help," and skulks off to the barn to put away his tools.

This is my first garden, ever. My mother grew flowers in front of our ranch, I remember that. Usually little prepotted plants we got at Prairie Gardens—impatiens, mostly. I remember their delicate pink and white petals; I never really liked the pink of them—there was something sort of dull or powdery about that pink, like Pepto Bismol. But I liked helping her drop the tight little bundles of roots into our small planter in front of our house. Sometimes, a sunflower or two would make its way in there. One year we got candy-striped petunias, after I read the book about Petunia, the goose who gets hold of some firecrackers.

When we're done gardening, the girls and I go and pick up prepacked boxes of groceries from the Co-Op in Blue Hill, our old Maine plates still bluffing for us. Every single drive, Duran Duran's "Hungry Like the Wolf" comes on the radio. The girls and I open all the windows and sing it at the top of our lungs. We all sort of hate the song by now, but we do it anyway. When I get out, I wear a cotton mask I bought on the honor system from a box at the end of someone's driveway. Now, we all have masks, more than one each. Cotton masks to keep in the car, medical masks I bought on Amazon to wear inside somewhere if we ever were to go inside somewhere. After our grocery run, we come back here to eat lunch and plan the next phase of our day.

Most days, I fill up Iris's little pink backpack with water bottles and rice cakes and oat bars and the girls and I hike along the beach looking for crabs under the wet, cool seaweed and periwinkles to pick up and hum to, pulling our shorts off and jumping into the water when we get hot, then continuing on until we can't walk any farther and Iris needs me to carry her on my back. Even in the rain, this plan does not get old for Iris; she would spend every day of her life along that coast, looking under seaweed, gazing up at osprey. Will sharks make this impossible?

"You're more likely to get in a car accident on the way to the Co-Op," says Pete. "Or get Covid. You and the girls can swim in the water, I think."

Some days, we meander up through the woods to the west and make our way to our favorite spot—a soft, pillowy place under a big white pine where we can sit and open the backpack and have a snack.

In the green of the evening, Runty comes sniffing, and as soon as he sees us go inside, he starts eating our lettuce. "Runty!" I shout out the kitchen window. "Get out of there." He looks at me impassively. I rattle the window and he runs.

Iris glares at me. "You always blame everything on Runty."

"He's annoying. Like you, dummy," pipes up Sophie.

"You have hair on your vulva!" retorts Iris, wiggling with the joy of hurling this fact of life at Sophie. How long has she been waiting for the right moment for this?

"Shut up, stupid," says Sophie.

"I saw you naked this morning. You have fur on your pee-pee like the fur on Mommy."

"Iris, stop it," I intervene. Just as I walk toward her to get down on her level so I can get her attention, Sophie lunges and pulls Iris's hair. Iris is shrieking and her feet and arms are going all akimbo and she's kicking at the bowls on the bottom shelf of the kitchen island. A blue bowl I love falls and shatters. "Girls!" I shriek. But Sophie is holding Iris down and punching her, saying between clenched teeth, "Shut. Up. Dummy! I hate you!" and now I'm yelling, "Iris, stop it. Sophie, stop! You just broke a bowl. Goddammit!"

Sophie shoves Iris down one more time against the hard floor and I hear Iris's head smack into the wood. Sophie's up then and off to her room, slamming the door as she yells, "I hate all of you!"

To which I yell back, "Gosh darnit, you two! What a mess!

"Iris, are you okay?" I ask, trying to soften, as my role requires, but I'm so worked up that even this attempt comes out angrily and from between clenched teeth. She looks at me, hurt; my anger is an abandonment. I breathe and try again: "Want to go get in the bath with a Magic Treehouse book on my phone?"

"Okay, Mommy." She looks at me tearfully, like she's the victim of a heinous crime.

"Take my hand," I say, as much out of wanting to comfort her as my desire to keep her from bolting upstairs to throw open Sophie's door and start the chaos all over again. The chaos that cycles throughout the day, day after day after day.

When she is finally in the bath, I survey the mess. In a few short months, almost everything in our house is broken or cracked: TV remotes can't hold batteries anymore; lampshades are duct-taped back together; all but five mugs have lost their handles; a pair of crystal candlesticks that were a wedding present exploded when their candles were allowed to burn too close to the glass; the chrome toilet paper holder dangles from the wall in the downstairs bathroom; there is a hole in the wall over the couch in the living room where Iris hit it with the fireplace poker.

In the midst of this wreckage, Pete and I can't bear to touch our own cracks. When we do, I get so angry I want to physically hurt him. At least, most days, we have the sense to let it lie.

But my mind wanders. I wonder if he's texting or calling The Her. When he's outside at night doing his walking thing, or in the car running errands, I drive myself crazy looking for clues and find nothing but Pete coming home with groceries, no calls but mine on his phone, no texts but mine.

I don't know how to untie us. We are bound in a way that gives me no other option but to thrash around in some ugly pool of disbelief, wanting to believe, then flashes of forgiveness, until I have no more thrash left. Like an eel, caught in a net with no more fight, I expect I will resign. That seems like the natural course, even if I resent it. I still thrash. I still thrash.

Moments that knit us back together keep happening here in Maine, confusing some of the hard and angry feelings I carried up from the city in a little pouch inside my stomach.

I can tell it better this way: We took a break—all of us— one day and drove up along the coast and then hiked in to a stream not far away from here. It was sweltering hot. Even Pete needed to get away from the computer, the relentless news. I carried Iris's backpack full of sandwich makings: cheese, pepperoni, bread, mustard. Pete carried the water. We were alone on the trail, the trees still damp from the rain the night before, the trunks dark and fragrant. The ground was soft; rock ledges sticking out of the pine needles were glistening and steaming in the hot air. Under the trees it was cooler, but we were all so hot. We came along a stream that was wide and had rocks so the kids could hop from one to the next, Sophie up ahead, a bandanna around her neck. As the stream widened, we came to a deep, dark spot—a hole—in the middle of the stream and, above it, a waterfall. We decided to stop. Sophie stripped down to her sports bra and shorts and was in the hole, immediately cooling off, a huge smile spreading across her face. "Oh my God, Daddy." She laughed. "You gotta try this."

Iris was pulling off her shoes and stepping into the shallow water near the hole before I could get my backpack off. Pete was there on the edge.

"Iris. Stay right here in the shallow water," I heard him say.

I pulled out a blanket and was making sandwiches. I turned to reach into the backpack for the mustard, and there was a splash. I looked up and saw Pete come rising out of the hole, fully clothed, hiking boots on, holding Iris, water peeling off him. Iris was crying, terrified.

With one look at Pete's face, he told me everything: ten, twenty seconds more, and she would have been gone.

He had both our phones, his wallet, his face mask, and his keys in his pockets. Phones were dead, wallet soaked. Who cares?

When we got back that night and Iris was finally in bed, I lay down next to her, as I do every night, to help her fall asleep. In the dark, her rush of tears came.

"I might have died, Mommy."

"I know," I said.

"Daddy saved me."

"I know."

"I hate myself for doing that."

"No, you must only learn. Never hate yourself. You need to be careful; do what we tell you. You are very impulsive. You could get hurt if you aren't more careful."

"What would have happened if I'd died?"

"We'd never recover."

"Sophie hates me."

"No, she doesn't. She loves you. She just doesn't know how to tell you that as often as you need to hear it."

"I don't want to die."

"No."

"Are you going to die?"

"Not for a long time. You don't need to worry about that right now."

"Are the polar bears dying? I heard you talking to Daddy."

Fresh tears. Hot and full of grief that is now like a tidal wave, cresting over both of us. My own face is slick.

"I don't know what will happen to the polar bears."

"Is someone going to kill all the sharks?"

Ah, my child. Absorbing things she hears me say on the phone to Sadie or to Pete in the kitchen with those extendable ears. She parrots my words back, making me uncomfortable. "Bad mother," I say to myself, shame tightening my stomach.

"No one will kill all the sharks. That would be impossible. And dangerous! We need the entire ecosystem to thrive. Most people understand that," I lie. In my mind I think, God, how can they not want to save all this? And then, who is the "they"?

Iris interrupts this confusing thought, where I'm now trapped in a loop. "Is everything going to die, Mommy?"

"At some point, everything dies. What we need to do now, as a world, is take our grief and try to save what we can. Like Noah. Remember Noah? That's what we will do. One by one. Now, it's time to sleep. But tomorrow we will save something—a bug, a butterfly, a bee—we'll make some small gesture. And the day after that another one. And maybe these will all add up, okay?"

"Okay. Mommy?"

"Yes?"

"Sophie says you shouldn't ever have married Daddy. That Daddy is going to leave us here in Maine soon."

"Daddy isn't going anywhere."

"Should you have married Daddy?"

"Without Daddy I wouldn't have you."

"Mommy, can you sleep with me tonight?"

"I'm right here. When you're asleep I'll go brush my teeth and come back. Deal?"

"Good night, Mommy."

"Go to sleep, Pickle."

When she was finally asleep, her breath hot and skin sticky against mine, I was thinking about summers in the city: taking

Sophie to her ballet class in the hot mornings, as she dragged her feet next to me, as I pushed Iris in her stroller, the pavement warming up to unbearable by the time Iris and I turned around and headed home. I remember the heat and how Pete was always working or gone and I was always annoyed at him for working or being gone.

After brushing my teeth and putting on my pj's, I went back to Iris's bed to slide in next to her. Pete was still up and working. Some nights I don't bother to say good night. As I lay next to her in the darkness I heard fluttering by the window. When I got up, I found a moth the size of a silver dollar trying to get out. Carefully, I cupped my hands around it, making a bowl with my palms so that I wouldn't rub the delicate powder off its wings. It was so soft, I noticed. And furry like Ingmar's nose. "Goodbye," I told it as I opened the window and set it free. "Stay safe." And after it was gone, I felt embarrassingly emotional. "Darn hormones," I said, swatting at the damp around my eyes.

When I got back into the bed, lying as straight as I could and trying not to touch Iris's hot, sticky body, I thought of a poem I read once. I've forgotten the name of it or where I read it but I remember the last line: "Lie up, and survive." That's it: lie up, survive, lie up, survive, lie up, survive. I think, We are all still here, we can all still tell each other what is happening to us, even as the polar bears die, even as sharks swim north, even as I thrash about in the murk of endings, near and far.

# 7

...

# Resilience

In *On the Banks of Plum Creek*, the Minnesota prairie stretches wide and tall around the Ingalls family's dugout house. There are fish in the stream and friends for the girls to play with, and, for a time, the family is happy. By then, the Ingallses have long ago left their magical little house in the big woods, left everything and everyone they knew, traveled far to the prairie, where they have battled fires and wind and terrible blizzards, until they are forced to leave by the government, which has decided to give back some stolen land to the Native Americans. The Ingallses then make their way to Minnesota. In Plum Creek, the land is luscious and giving for a time. This was before the grasshoppers, before scarlet fever, before Mary went blind.

Iris hears her mother tell her that the Ingalls family is *resilient*, that is the word she uses, during hardship, that they stand strong. Iris asks Alice what that means, and Alice explains that they endure "hard things," and that "they never assume their lives should be easy," and "they work at living, even when it's challenging." She reminds Iris of the time Laura and Mary bring the entire woodpile into the house during a blizzard when Ma and Pa are in town.

"Are we resilient?" asks Iris as she picks at a scab on her elbow, making it bleed.

"I think so," says Alice, now absent-minded, having lost the fervor she held on to briefly as she explained the Ingallses to her daughter. Iris wants to hear her mother say, "Yes, we are, very." But Iris knows enough about mothers by now, or her mother, anyway, to know that mothers don't always do just what you want; they have secret thoughts of their own. Iris finds this disturbing. She wants her mother to know exactly what she is thinking, to feel what she is feeling, to understand what she means *inside*, without having to utter a peep. She wants her mother to have *her* feelings and thoughts, and when she perceives her mother might be somewhere in her own locked room of thoughts and not paying close attention, Iris is uncomfortable. It's like a disappearance.

Later, when Iris asks her mother again, "Are we resilient?" Alice will understand and say, "Of course we are." And then, "Look how we've done this, how we're hanging together during this pandemic, look at our lives in Maine."

But today, as they are cuddled in her bed, Iris notices that her mother has drifted off to look, dreamily, out the window. Her mother has become quiet. Iris has to knock the book and say, not gently, "Mama! Weed!" She means *read*, but her *r*'s have sounded like *w*'s since she was three and it's never changed except with intense concentration to make an *r* sound like an *r*.

Alice tells Iris about how the land in Minnesota has been carved up now, how there are strip malls. She tells Iris about how she used to go out her back door in her suburban neighborhood, and that there was a field behind the house, and she used to wander back there imagining she was Laura, her own two pigtails bouncing against her back as she ran through the tall grasses. Now, there's a Staples and an Arby's there, Alice tells Iris. "That Arby's is so close that when the wind is right, if my parents open their windows they can smell roast beef–and–cheese sandwiches. Isn't that silly?" she says, but Iris can tell that her mother doesn't feel it's silly, really; just sad.

Alice uses the books to explain the extermination of Native Americans. She tries to explain Ma's fears of the land, the wolves, the "Indians" in the context of the time, and what it was like for Ma to follow her husband with her precious children out into the great unknown. She explains the relief Ma feels when they finally get to Minnesota, after the fear she felt on the prairie. Alice talks about the differences between now and then and how women were just expected to follow their husbands; that men didn't follow their wives. She talks about the Trail of Tears and sometimes Alice cries and then Iris cries. "Is there anything we can do to help?" she asks.

"This was a long time ago," says Alice. "I need to think about that."

Iris asks, "But what about that one Native American who is stealing from Ma in the *Little House on the Prairie* book? And why in the drawing are both Native Americans stealing when Laura says it was only the one?"

"I don't know," Alice says. "The artist got that wrong, didn't he?" And then they look at the drawing with the two Native Americans stealing and Alice rereads to Iris the moment when Laura asks Pa what is happening.

*"Will the government make these Indians go west?"*

*"Yes," Pa said. "When white settlers come into a country, the Indians have to move on. The government is going to move these Indians farther west, any time now. That's why we're here, Laura. White people are going to settle all this country, and we get the best land because we get here first and take our pick. Now do you understand?"*

*"Yes, Pa," Laura said. "But, Pa, I thought this was Indian Territory. Won't it make the Indians mad to have to—"*

*"No more questions, Laura," Pa said, firmly. "Go to sleep."*

"Are we allowed to settle *here*?" asks Iris.

"Oh, sure. It's America. We can go anywhere we want."

"Anyone can?"

"Well, mostly."

"But there were those people, the ones with the chain saws—"

"That was just Covid politics, honey."

"Are there still wolves on the prairie?"

"Not many. I don't know. Not many, I guess. Now it's bedtime for you—let's not think about the Trail of Tears or wolves or Ma and Pa and three little girls on the prairie anymore. Until tomorrow, okay?"

"Can I go get Ingmar?"

"You need a cuddle?"

Iris nods, solemn as a priest.

"Run along. Pee first."

Iris comes back holding tightly to Ing, his long body trailing almost the length of hers, his feet skidding over the floor. She squeezes him a little too tightly under his shoulders and he looks the slightest bit panicked as she crawls into bed, still holding him, and shoves him under the covers next to her, now pinning him down as she cups her body around his.

"Good night, sweetie. Good night, Ing," Alice says almost breezily.

Iris notices that her mother seems distracted. Ready to go downstairs. Ready to go down and fight with Daddy, she thinks to herself. She squeezes more tightly to Ing. But Ingmar uses his bottom paws to push against her, and scuttles down under the covers and off the bed. Iris feels alone and wants to go to her mother. But she worries that she might find her parents fighting or her mother crying, or, even worse, that cold silence that sometimes descends, and things feel very ominous. So she scrunches down the covers and peeks her eyes just over the top. Like this, finally, she falls asleep.

When Iris goes outside the next morning, she carries the old rusty Swiss Army knife she found in the barn in her hand and likes the feeling of her blue-flowered dress swishing around her calves; she likes imagining it's a "calico," and under her baseball cap, she has had her mother braid her hair into two long pigtails. Outside, she doesn't think about Staples and Arby's or Indian Territory. She sees a huge field of grasses and black-eyed Susans around her little house on the shore of a great ocean, and she can pretend she's on the prairie. She can pretend she is surviving with her *resilient* family far away from everything they know. And in a way she is, they are.

After the almost-drowning incident she isn't allowed anywhere near the beach alone. And so Iris asks Pete to cut her blocks of sod bricks. Pete goes out with an old shovel and digs from somewhere in the middle of their field and brings the bricks back, one by one. She notices how the dirt falls over his arms and how she's not sure she's ever seen her father with his hands in the earth before. Each block has at its base a mystery of tangled roots and bugs scrambling for safety and worms writhing about. She holds each one over her head and peers into the dirty darkness, trying to catch a glimpse of an inner life. "Here ya go, E. O.," her father says. He's taken to calling her E. O., he tells her, after some famous ant guy at Harvard, because she spends her entire days looking closely at ants and pill bugs and crabs. Iris arranges the sod blocks against one side of the barn into a sort of lean-to that she is able to get inside and pretend is her dugout house. She brings out a small broom and sweeps the floor and then she gathers plates and cups and stacks them on a brick and eats her lunch alone in the dirt hovel she has created for herself, watching the worms dangle and then tuck themselves back into the ceiling she's made above. The smell of earth and grass and the heat of the summer sun baking the fields is the best thing she can imagine. Iris wants time to stop.

And then she sees the bare feet of her sister. They seem very large, almost monstrous. There's some peeling purple polish on the nails of Sophie's big toes.

"What are you doing, Poop?" she hears Sophie's voice.

"Hiding," says Iris, though that's only partly true. And obviously not that well, since her sister has found her, since her father cut her the pieces of sod, since everyone knows where she is.

"You're weird," Sophie tells her sister.

Iris isn't that sure whether she is or isn't weird. Sometimes she talks to herself in funny little languages she makes up in her head and her brain feels like it can do anything, even see into the inner lives of creatures. She talks to the birds and bugs and deer on the edge of the meadow. Yesterday, there was a small flock of bluebirds in the lilac by the driveway, and Iris spoke to the two males and they shook their little tails and fluttered their feathers and squeaked and chittered in response.

When Iris thinks no one is looking and the world feels big around her and she feels very alone and quiet in it, she sometimes makes her way to a small stream that flows murkily down to the ocean to the south of their property. Rocks and trees border it, and even in the hot summer, Iris can lose herself in the cool shady patches. Closer to the ocean, there is a deeper pool carved out of the rocks. It only goes up to Iris's knees, so she feels it's not off-limits, though she hasn't asked. On her second trip, Iris discovered eight—she counted them—small eels squiggling through the water. She ran back breathless to the house, her face shining with her discovery. Her mother came along with her and together they sat on the edge of the pool looking in, watching the thin, translucent bodies pause but not exactly be still on the murky rocks. Alice told her later they were called elvers, and she read out loud to her parts of a book called *The Book of Eels*. Iris learned how they migrate by moonlight when they are fully grown but that they can live in streams for twenty or fifty or maybe it was a hundred years, Iris can't remember. Her mother told her they were a special thing, and she should feel lucky to find them in her stream.

Iris visits them on her regular rounds outside. The same blue dress, dirt on her knees, her cap pulled down on her brow to keep the sun out. She investigates the secret, watery indentations and holes along the grassy sides of the stream. There is something about the elvers, their wriggling quality, that reminds Iris of something deep inside herself, something she doesn't yet understand, something subtle and wiggly in the lower part of her belly. When she feels it, she wants to run around and stand on her head and do cartwheels until it passes.

One evening, Iris told Sophie in great detail everything she was learning about elvers, and Sophie only said, "That's great, dummy."

Iris was startled. "I thought you liked things like that, stories about animals."

"I just don't really care, dummy" was all Sophie said.

Ever since her sister started her period and they moved to Maine, some strange thing has happened between them. They appear to be diametrically opposed, though, of course, Iris would never use those words. Her sister has shifted away from her. It's not been so long that she can't remember them playing together, her sister's warm arm around her when they watched a show or a movie together, her sister teaching her to play Sleeping Queens on the old nubbly rug in their square playroom between their two rooms in their apartment in Manhattan. Iris used to love that open space filled with bookshelves and plants, a fish tank, and that blue wool rug; baskets of toys on the bottom shelves and along the wall and a big black chalkboard on one side. Across the hall, they had their own bathroom, where she could put her small, pink panties into the same hamper as Sophie's bigger pink panties and then satisfyingly put the top back on the hamper and feel that their private girl secrets were all in that little cluster of rooms, intermingled and bound up with each other.

Now Iris is not sure they are anymore, that any of the secrets Sophie has are her secrets or whether Sophie will ever tell her one of hers again. All she knows is that she misses her sister. But she can't find the words to tell her that, and so she annoys Sophie endlessly, which only seems to draw more and more contempt, and the chasm grows, beach dunes eroding into the sea.

Her mother tells her that her sister will come back around, that she loves her, that families go through tough periods and things happen and people stretch apart like they are at two ends of a rubber band and then they come back together. Whenever her mother says that, Iris imagines a big, thick, pink rubber band, like the kind that comes on broccoli from the grocery store, and she imagines two plastic people, like the kind that go on top of a cake, on either end, stretching between her fingers.

Now her sister's underwear sometimes has a red stain on it, and though Alice tells Iris that one day she will also have a red stain on her underwear, it still alarms her when she sees it. It does not explain how Sophie has gone from being her friend to now finding everything Iris does unbearably annoying. It does not explain how often Sophie tells Iris how stupid she is. It does not explain the lonely feeling Iris has inside.

After she fell into the deep pool and her dad went after her, when Iris came up for air and was gasping in the light that suddenly seemed in Technicolor, Iris saw her sister through the water that was streaming down her own face, and she saw a look of terror. Crying and still clutching her dad, Iris heard herself yelp out to Sophie, "You would have been glad if I died," and then felt herself cry harder. "I'll never not see it," she sobbed into her father's neck. She wasn't sure if he understood that she meant the light goldeny brown water and her hair floating up above her and the roar of the waterfall and what it was like to start to scream underwater as her body sank like a stone. She meant those four or five milliseconds that felt like four or five years when she was trying to call out, "Mama, Mama!" And then her dad had her first by the wrist and then under both arms and they were out in the sunlight, the glorious sunlight, and he was banging on her back, and the first face she saw was Sophie's, her beautiful, smart, capable, talented bigger sister.

Still weeping and going over and over the whole thing in her mind as she gripped her father and felt her mother's arm around her, she saw Sophie reach out and put her hand on her shoulder and she saw her sister's face close to hers. She saw Sophie's blue eyes and the freckles on her nose, and then she heard Sophie say, "Iris, I would be devastated if you drowned. I am glad you're okay."

*Devastated.* Such a big, important word. What does devastated look like? Iris wondered. What would her sister look like if she were devastated? What a responsibility, to have the power to devastate another person.

All Iris could do was weep against her father's wet shirt, the sun slowly warming her hair down her back.

# 8

• • •

# August

There was one night when Iris was a baby and screaming her colicky head off and not sleeping, and Pete was bouncing her on a big plastic exercise ball in the living room, trying to give me a break, when, as I was on my way to the bathroom, I heard his voice, frustrated and exhausted, say, "Jesus, Iris. No one will ever love you if you're like this." His voice sounded strangled, desperate. I went back to bed and felt myself get outraged, like this enormous mother lion was roaring inside my mind. No one? Not even us? What the fucking fuck, Pete! was all I could think. Somehow, lying there trying to calm down and stop myself from going out there and screaming, I must have fallen asleep. I was exhausted.

In the morning, I found Pete asleep on the couch with Iris

on his chest. She was drooling onto his old red Rolling Stones T-shirt, the one with Mick's mouth, and making a wet pool over his heart. For a minute, as I stood over them, like some sort of weird henchman, I felt a microburst of that hailstorm, the fire-and-brimstone anger that had coursed through me in the night. I wanted to give Pete the finger in his face, to gnash my teeth and punch his slack, defenseless face.

Except there he was, cuddled with our little, delicate, exhausting daughter, who was peaceful for the first time in God knows how many days. And somehow, the storm inside me changed to a soft, nurturing rain, and I realized that I had, thanks to Pete, gotten the first good sleep in a long time, ever since Iris was born. He had said what he had said. But nevertheless, here Iris was, happily asleep on his chest, and his big, dark hairy arm was holding on to her like a life raft.

In Maine, as the large pool of what's not being discussed seems to grow more stinky and repugnantly coated with a fast-growing and slithery algae, and as the marooned limbo life-is-on-hold feeling settles over every waking hour that we are suspended here, I go back to that moment. Even after Pete and I have sex. Even when things should be fine but aren't fine.

In those moments, when he's asleep, thinking things are getting back to fine, or maybe he's even happy, I don't know, I try to put a finger on when things broke between Pete and me. I realize it wasn't entirely the anxiety he elicited in me with his extroverted and charming way with people. It wasn't even the strange disembodiment that happened when I couldn't finish that second play and went on to have Sophie, and the writing and theater worlds and all my ambition seemed to evaporate along with the milk Sophie drained from my breasts overnight. It wasn't my shock that I had become stuck, despite all the education and ambition that once defined me. It wasn't the dingy feeling, specifically, that suddenly appeared in my psyche and made me feel that I was lost in the big city, lost as a wife, as a mother, unsure of who I was anymore. And it wasn't, if I am honest, when I found out about The Her.

No, the trouble, the schism, really happened when I began worrying that Pete didn't love Iris as desperately as I did. Didn't want her like I did.

Iris was a difficult baby, to say the least. She was a tiny, red-faced preemie who screamed her head off most of the time, making us all crazy. She rejected nannies and babysitters, howling even when I tried to hand her to Pete.

After two miscarriages, I had been sure I'd never have another child; I assumed my body was done with this ancient ritual, had closed up shop. Pete had come around to the idea that one child was better for us. Or him anyway. "It's enough to figure out how to take care of and love Sophie," he'd said. And then, miraculously, I had gotten pregnant with Iris and something settled in our universe, like we had landed on the right little strip of desert with an oasis nearby.

I was huge—I mean huge—and very healthy the entire pregnancy, with no problems. I thought about my body as lovely swollen fruit on a vine, something I should care for tenderly. And then, without warning, at thirty-four weeks, just before Halloween, labor began. Pangs of pain were radiating across my uterus like lightning slicing through a dark summer sky. I left Sophie with our neighbor, old lady Eleanor, and rushed to the hospital. Pete appeared in his blue suit and white shirt, no tie—I remember that. And I remember how handsome he looked, his tan neck against the white of his shirt and the deep evening blue of the suit, his dark hair cut short. It was still warm outside, "a real Indian summer," as my mother used to say, and he looked so fresh and strong. He rolled up his sleeves to help and his strong forearms grounded me.

When Iris came out, she was a tiny slip of a thing, barely four and a half pounds. She'd required almost no pushing and certainly no Pitocin. Iris's body was cool and bluish and crumpled-looking, like a hairless baby mouse. Immediately she was whisked away by the nurses, who said something was wrong. I can never remember if they said, "She's not breathing," or "She's not breathing right," or "There's a problem," or what the hell they said. Pete says it was none of those things, it was some sort of nurse language like "Her blood oxygen is low," or something that we didn't understand yet were able to grasp the gist of. They ran out of the room with her, and then I was screaming and Pete was trying to hold me and telling me they would save her and I was trying to get up to follow my baby, to run after them, and he was saying no, to let them do their job, and I can't remember anything more except just one long, horrible howl inside my chest, tearing me apart. I have no idea if any of it was out loud or silent or what.

When I saw my baby again, she was in the NICU, hooked up to tubes and machines. Pete was leaning into her clear plastic bassinet, one finger clasped in Iris's teeny-tiny hand. He looked exhausted, wrinkled. His shirt no longer looked so bright white, and what seemed tan and vibrant before now looked dingy and gray. This is going to undo us, I thought.

For the first month of her tiny life, I stayed with Iris in the hospital, unwilling to go home. I barely showered. Pete brought me turkey, cheese, bread, and mayonnaise and put them in a little kitchen. When Iris was sleeping I went in there and made sandwiches. I ate two or three at a time, shoving them into my mouth in gulps, swallowing, repeating. I lay on a cot next to my daughter, watching the green lights of the monitors measuring Iris's oxygen and heart rate until I couldn't keep my eyes open. I got up every time her diaper needed to be changed or she was hungry. When I slept, I felt like I was walking on the edge of a cliff and had let go of Iris's hand. At any moment Iris might plummet down a steep bank to an ocean, green and roiling below.

Pete came and went in a blur—lunch breaks, with Sophie after school, Saturday mornings with a bag of doughnuts. I noticed my husband and first daughter arriving and leaving, hugging and kissing me, *needing* me, but they were fuzzy around the edges, more like mirages of something I was trying to swim or crawl back to, only they were too far off.

At first, in those dim first hours or days—who knows now, it all felt like eons and seconds—when they told me Iris might not be able to suckle, I pumped my milk. But I was determined she would nurse. I did everything I could glean from the nurses and find on the internet. I hunched over my baby, my breast in my hand, trying and trying, and then, finally, blessedly, Iris's little mouth settled on my nipple like a latch, and we were bound together.

The NICU was another land altogether, another planet. Everything there—the babies in plastic bassinets everywhere, the flashing lights and beepers, and the disoriented looks on the faces of the parents—it was unlike anywhere I had ever been before, this hidden world I knew nothing about. It was like, I imagine, going to a war or having a near-death experience; I felt like the molecules in my body got rearranged while I was there into something different from people who had never been in the NICU. The NICU was my band of babies and nurses and mothers and fathers and I was never going to forget it or them.

There was a tall thin nurse, with a sharp face, a brusque manner, and red hair, whom I came to name Dolores, for the novel *Dolores Claiborne*. I could never remember her real name in the chaos and exhaustion of that month, so Dolores stuck in my head. One night, I came upon Dolores trying to change Iris's diaper. I had been in the bathroom. And Dolores was holding Iris's tiny legs up like a chicken that she was trussing, and there was this casual, impersonal roughness to the way she held Iris, as if Iris weren't someone's daughter, she was a job, a thing. I was immediately furious. Standing over them, I had to control myself from hitting her hands away, from leaping at her and tearing her apart. Likely growling, I said, "Only I change her diaper. Let go." One look told me how much Dolores would hate me from then on. But I didn't care. She could come break my ankles later if she wanted.

"You'll be exhausted," Dolores snorted and picked up Iris. "Making yourself do everything when we're right here. And you'll never make any milk if you make yourself this tired. She'll get a feeding tube. Formula." In my head I said, Fuck off. To Dolores I said, "Thank you," and gave her my cold "Don't fuck with me" smile. Don't get me wrong. This isn't an anti-nurse diatribe. I knew I needed the nurses—even that horrible Dolores—to help Iris survive. The nurses saved her. Without them, without the hospital, if we'd been stuck out on the prairie in 1890, forget it. That's one thing that's not in those *Little House* books—the babies that Ma lost. But I would be damned if any one of them would replace what I—Iris's mother, for God's sake—could do. "I know how to change a diaper," I said. "I'd be doing that at home, wouldn't I?" And I said, "I am the mother. I will do everything that is required of me in that role. You do what is required of you."

There was one horrible and long night that I will never forget. The nurses had insisted upon moving an IV from Iris's tiny hand to her head in the middle of the night for the last few hours of a hospital-regulated antibiotic. It was a gruesome scene; they couldn't get the IV into her head and Iris was screaming. And then I was screaming at them to stop, that this was not necessary, that we were talking about three hours, for Chrissake. But the nurses had this set look, that they would bend this baby to what was required, regulations were regulations. They banished me from the room, put me in some other strange room with orange walls and a small cot, where I paced like a lion in the zoo and called Pete and wailed at the injustice, the chaos, of the whole thing. When I came back, Iris was trembling, and her cry-ing sounded like an animal caught in a trap. Her body was cold to the touch, and she was shivering and wouldn't stop. I undid my shirt and held Iris against my bare chest and draped blankets over us and held her all night, my eyes wide open. Something had happened to us there, something significant, something that would register in her small body and perhaps mine too, as some kind of torture, no matter the intention. We could never go back; we'd been forever changed by this land of beeps and computers and nurses and babies.

When Dolores came on for the late shift that night, I re-lented: I would need to make friends with her. I was all alone. And I needed someone to tell if Iris got worse, someone who could help. All I had was a bag of clementines my friend Molly had brought me. I offered Dolores a clementine, of all things. And she took it, and ate it, the orange juicing between her white teeth. "Thank you," Dolores said, her mouth pursed from the acid pleasure of the fruit. That night she didn't lecture me or scare me. She just worked around me as I sat up, holding Iris, my baby's long cords snaking back to all kinds of things I didn't understand.

"Do something," I told Pete on the phone that night. And I believe he tried. There was a guy he worked with, one of the major shareholders, who was on the board of the hospital. Pete called him and asked for something, maybe a senior doctor, a special room, anything, he would tell me later. I do remem-ber a man in green scrubs who came from somewhere else in the hospital and arrived in this separate country of the NICU.

He descended officiously into the room and told me he was so-and-so, the chief of something. I remember he stood with his legs far apart, and he waggled a bit as he talked, swinging his hips, and I imagined his balls jiggling underneath his scrubs. His tone was slightly sanctimonious, imperious, down here in this tropical country of nurses and women and babies. I remember his smooth, tan skin of privilege and his blond hair and his devastatingly blue eyes, and that he said something like "We are doing everything we can, everything we are required to do. It's better to let us do what we need to do."

"Okay" was all I said.

And then, just as he was leaving, he said, "It's unusual. Most of these kids are left in here. We barely see the parents. And when we do, the parents are drunk or high."

Later, when Pete came to the hospital, he arrived with Joan and Richard. I remember the sleek way Richard's black cashmere overcoat swished, the silk lining making a snakelike whisper as it rubbed against his designer jeans and the charcoal gray sweater that covered a sky-blue oxford. I remember his shiny leather loafers and gray cashmere socks, and that he was wearing a cravat in navy blue, and that his hair looked thick and white and luxurious. Joan's gold bracelets clacked against the bassinet where Iris was sleeping when she peered in to look. At some point during that visit, another man arrived, also in a suit, and Pete and his father and the man stood outside in the hall, out of earshot, while Joan and I were left to sit staring at little Iris, one hand of mine woven underneath all the tubes to allow her to hold my pinky in her tiny pink hand. "This will be okay," Joan said, arranging her long black, gauzy sweater. "You are safe. Richard will take care of this."

The man in the suit left after shaking hands with Pete and his father, and after that, the blond man with the steel blue eyes and the jiggly balls under his greens scrubs came and checked on me once more, asking if I needed anything. By then I had realized that all I could do, all Iris could do, was endure, lie up, survive. There was nothing more to do and that was no one's fault. It just was what it was.

But there was Diane, a large, dark-haired nurse with steady hands who worked mornings. She had this really gentle voice, and when she arrived, after yet another night spent watching the computer screen that registered Iris's oxygen levels and heartbeat, I could feel my shoulders go down a bit. "Rest," she said. "I can't," I told her. I remember one morning Diane put her hand softly on my back and said, "The worst is almost over. She is growing. She is breathing on her own. It was just the shock of it all. She will be okay. You will go home soon, I promise. You have done so well, taken such good care."

My mother came all the way from Minneapolis to stay with Pete and Sophie so that Pete could go back to work. My mother had never come alone to New York before. But she came this time. She was confused by the busy streets and the subway, making it harder for Pete. She didn't feel comfortable hailing a cab and bringing Sophie to see Iris and me. Sophie had to wait until Pete got home from work, and he would bring my exhausted and often hungry five-year-old to get a quick hug from me before dinner and bed. One night, Pete appeared with Sophie wearing a little bright-red beret, her blond hair in a mussy braid down her back. Sophie bounced and grabbed at things in the room, pointed to the lights, and chattered too much. Pete began to raise his voice at her and picked her up to admonish her, holding her firmly as she looked away. I asked, "Has anyone fed her a snack since school?"

Pete looked at Sophie sharply. "Did Grannie feed you anything, honey?"

"No," said Sophie, now on the verge of tears herself.

"Jesus Christ, Pete."

"Sophs, let's go down to the cafeteria," he said wearily, but not unkindly. I saw his shoulders slump in a way I had never seen before. Later, I would think, That was the moment I could have somehow reached out, told him we would be okay. But it was like I was dried up inside. There was nothing more to give anyone other than this tiny child on my breast, whom I desperately needed to survive. And all I felt inside was empty.

Late at night, Pete would call me to complain. "Jesus, I need to take care of your mom so she can take care of Sophie," Pete said.

My mother was a chore. I understood this. For the last several years she seemed to be showing early signs of dementia. Or maybe it was just old age? I don't know. Whatever it was, it was fucking irritating. She was blank when she really should not be, it seemed to me. But if I thought back, she had been, for years now, one of those people who felt scared and unsure of everything, never seeming competent. She liked to be in her own little world, going to the grocery store, playing bridge with her friends, making coffee, walking around the high school track, making macramé. She had never been incredibly adventurous. It was my dad who brought the adventure into the family, the sense that there was air around us, possibility.

After that year he was gone, when my dad eventually came home, my mother never went back to his office. She still baked and cleaned and walked every day and made our dinner. She still played bridge. We still had pizza on Thursday nights and my father still regaled Brian and me with stories while my mother retired early with a book. I wouldn't see her again until the morning. This became kind of normal, expected, as things do.

"Pete, it's better than nothing," I said. "She does laundry and dishes while you're gone, right?"

"Yes, I guess. But she puts the colors with the whites. Sometimes I'm not sure she's even used soap. She piles the dirty dishes all over the counter in some sort of chaos I don't understand. And when she finally does load the dishwasher and wash the pots and pans and larger spoons, she spreads them to dry everywhere—even the dining table. I honestly think she spends the whole time I'm gone and Sophie's in school brushing Ingmar. He looks better than ever. She feeds him all the time, plays with him. Those two are inseparable."

I wanted to say but didn't say because I was too tired to fight, "At least my mother is good for that. Making sure the cat is still alive by the time I come home."

When Iris and I finally did come home and my mother had departed, Iris refused to be put down. If you tried, she screamed bloody murder. She slept in a hot, matted heap on my chest and screamed most of her waking hours, no matter what I did. I took gluten, dairy, spicy foods, soy, beans, corn, cabbage, and kale—anything that might be causing Iris gas—out of my diet and had no idea what to eat anymore. I was starving, it felt like. But nothing worked. Iris still screamed. At the advice of a counselor sent through the hospital, I began taking painstaking notes of everything I ate and when Iris slept, of how long her naps were, of what times of day Iris screamed bloody murder. I was desperate to find patterns, answers.

*IRIS SLEEP:*

*monday:*
*8:25—9:04 (on my chest)*
*10:15—10:47 (in bed)*
*12:15—1:50 (in moby)*
*5:13—5:40 (stroller)*
*bedtime 8:30.*

*i lost count of how many times she woke up.*

*tuesday:*
*7:30—9:00 (in bed with me)*
*11:00—11:40 (stroller)*

*no later nap. screamed all afternoon. i had a decaf today. last night i ate cheese?*

It took Iris and me an hour to walk the fifteen minutes it would normally take to pick up Sophie from school, five blocks away. We had to stop on every corner so I could take Iris out of the stroller and crouch on a stoop to nurse until she was calm enough to continue. It felt like it would never end. Sophie, in kindergarten then, made herself quieter and asked less of me. She was folding inward and I didn't know what to do. I had no idea how to change the course we were on.

Pete was short-fused almost constantly. Our lives had been fine, easy, with just Sophie. And now this red-faced screaming bundle, who came too early, too expensively, had forced him to cohabitate with my addled mother for a month, and now didn't let anyone sleep. Pete left for work exhausted, came home exhausted. His magnetic, strong, virile self, the one that drew other people to him like moths through a lighted window, had dimmed. I could see that. But I couldn't find the time, the strength, the whatever was needed to reach out and help him.

I kept assuming that the sleeping troubles would end at six months, a year, two, and I would find the time then to reconnect with Sophie, and, after that, with Pete. But time wore on and Iris's inability to sleep through the night persisted. Pete and I were never in our bed alone together. Iris could not sleep without matting herself against my chest, kneading my stomach for comfort. I was stuck in the bedroom every night, soothing, rocking, holding, and then finally falling into a drugged and anxious sleep myself. Pete had started napping in the middle of the day at work and staying up late at night, catching up after he did the dinner cleanup, set up Sophie's backpack for the next day, and paid bills. It was a lonely time. I thought I'd swim back to Sophie and Pete but it was like I was being pulled by a riptide I couldn't get out of.

I knew enough to realize I needed help. That was when I found Lois. Lois understood that I could only see her every two weeks because the demands of mothering Iris and Sophie were too great to afford me much time to investigate what was happening inside my head. "This is that time of life," Lois said, her gray hair neatly tucked behind her dangly silver earrings with little boulders of turquoise hanging at the ends. "It won't last forever. Let us begin."

When Iris was finally five, just before I knew about The Her, before the Covid problem, before Maine, she began sleeping through the night. It was only for a short period. A few weeks, maybe a month. Enough to notice the difference with a kind of shock in the early morning that felt disarming. I quickly got up to check to make sure Iris was still in her bed, that she was still breathing.

Those nights that Pete and I had the bed to ourselves, we fought. This window was given to us, and in the letdown, we argued. And then I slept like I was making up for a hundred years of no sleep. Though it's possible Pete reached out for me in the night, I was too exhausted to notice or even care. I felt like a swimmer tired out, waterlogged.

Looking back now, I wonder about all that—the fighting, my exhaustion, what Pete was doing in a life he was living in secret, away from us—that strange time when we could have swum back to each other but didn't.

One morning, in the first days of March, I picked up Pete's phone when he was in the shower. Usually already done with his shower when I'm barely awake, this morning he was running late. Covid was just beginning to sweep over the city and we had been up past midnight, talking and watching the news. School hadn't been closed yet, but I thought both kids should stay home. Pete didn't think we were there, that it hadn't become a crisis. Oh, how little we knew! Later, he would remember some of the unusual market activity in February and realize that not only was it already with us, but that the White House had known and done nothing. I remember him telling me that.

But this morning both kids needed breakfast and I was moving sluggishly.

I was tidying our bed as I tried to rouse myself when I found Pete's phone peeking out from under his pillow and I saw a text from someone named just "S." It read, Meet you later at our usual spot? Front desk has the keycard . . . My nipples are already hard. This was followed by several—was it five?—red and pink emoji lips.

I didn't need to think. I walked into the bathroom with his phone and opened the shower curtain. I remember he leapt back, naked, his penis swinging, and one part of me felt empathy, another revulsion. "What. The. Fuck. Is. This?" And then I threw the phone into the shower at him as hard as I could, hitting him not in his softest, most vulnerable spot, but, regrettably, in the thigh. I heard the phone bang against the tile floor as I left the bathroom, slamming the door. I was shaking.

Then, like I had taken speed or drunk three hundred coffees, I got both kids dressed and took them to the corner diner for an egg on a kaiser roll, and then to school. My phone remained off. I walked for hours that day—through Central Park all the way past Columbia, stopping briefly at Absolute Bagels to get an everything bagel with the slightly sweet pickle-and-carrot tuna salad that I crave and only allow myself to have every so often with a cup of black coffee. Holding my paper cup in one hand, the bagel in the other, I kept walking: through Morningside, then back down through Riverside. There were moments when my outrage dulled to a strange feeling of freedom—when was the last time I had spent a whole day walking? When was the last time I spent this many hours thinking my own thoughts, even miserable thoughts? When I got home, I was shivering and cold and Pete was waiting for me.

If you ask me now what happened that day, I can't remember all of it, honestly. Except that it was dismal. I remember flying at Pete and hitting him in the face with my fist. I remember dishes smashing, shoes exploding out of their neat little lines in the entryway. I remember the way Ingmar ran out of the room, ears back, tail down. I remember Pete packing his gym duffel bag as I screamed a long barrage of words that may not even have been words, it occurs to me now. I remember feeling scared that he was leaving, angry that he was leaving, glad that he was leaving. I remember how he roared back at me about the five long years when I would barely touch him, that I was in some sort of weird fucking fog of emotional chaos after Iris. I roared back, "Do you have any idea how much I have given up to be a mother and wife? How dare you blame this on me! You've always been like this. I've seen it for years. I knew you would cheat. I never *ever* should have married you."

I remember he left with a sickening click of the door, and that

I texted him as I heard the elevator open down the hall: Do not call me. I will call you. Do not come back. I swept up the broken dishes. I straightened the shoes. I found Ingmar and held him, pressing my face into his fur as I cried. And then I showered. I had to pick up our children and bring them home. Even then I was cognizant of the reality that they were going to be in a small apartment with an emotionally unhinged mother.

I don't remember how we did it. I think I was shaking much of the time. I do remember holding them to me, breathing them in, their clean, soft, little-girl smell.

For that first week both girls slept in my bed with me. Sophie did ask, "Where is Daddy?" Iris stood wide-eyed.

"Working," I said. "Away."

"When will he be back?"

"I don't know," I said, unable to shield my children as much as I should, as I wanted to be strong enough to do. "Sometimes big people have trouble loving each other the right way. I can't say any more, Sophs. I don't want to say something that would be the wrong thing to say. Okay? I love you. I am here. You are safe. Daddy will come back." After a moment, I tried to say more. "He will be fine."

I really didn't know. I heard nothing. Our bills continued to debit automatically, our phones stayed on, money came into our bank account that Thursday, everything proceeded as if it were all perfectly normal and no cataclysm had eventuated anywhere but inside my chest. The kids and I ate as best we could. But Pete was gone and nothing and everything had changed. Was he staying with The Her? Sleeping at his desk? How many of our friends knew? What friends of his had looked me in the face and known all along? Their wives too? I was not going to call him; many women had done harder things. I was capable, I told myself, even though I felt not one bit capable.

In the end, Pete wasn't gone long. After just over a week, he appeared at the door. It was dinnertime, and I was trying to feed the kids frozen organic Tilapia fish sticks, frozen tater tots, and sliced tomatoes from some water-hungry place in Mexico. Three days in, I had stopped cooking. I could not. I could barely load the dishwasher. Feeding Ingmar hurt my soul. Feeding myself was torture. Every little thing felt painful, like needles were pricking me all over. My marriage, as far as I could tell, was over, and perhaps at the same time the world was ending, as this tsunami virus was cresting and about to flatten us all. The timing of it made me sick with worry.

It was evening, and the girls could hear him there at the door. He had planned it that way, I was sure: having the girls home gave him some insurance. In the doorway he said, "We'll have to figure it out. The virus. It isn't safe. We need to be a family. I'm not leaving my girls. The other thing is over."

"Ha!" was all I said. Crazy angry was back.

"Please, Alice. I will fix it." He put his hand on the door, holding it.

And then he came in. I didn't speak. What was there to say? I had said it all the day I flew at him. All words had been wrung out of me. And now it was so simple—I just stood aside and back into our lives he walked. No time had passed; a week is nothing. He'd been gone on business trips longer than that. With the virus and everything there had been no time to even think about what was happening. To take stock. To talk.

First Pete slept on the couch, but that became scary to Sophie, who was having horrible nightmares about us all dying. She would wake up in the middle of the night to come find me, and Pete was not in the bed, which alarmed her. She was afraid he was sick or dead and would start crying, even when I said he was just sleeping in the living room. Within two days, Pete was sleeping back in the bed, Iris in the middle, and some nights, even Sophie dangling off one edge.

Mashed together there was no space to say anything or to even calm my heart. I lay awake, the children and Pete snoring and Iris's little body hot against my skin. My mind bounced like popcorn in a hot pan from the virus to my marriage to my kids to the world, and back again to start all over. I would spiral into feelings of violence that alarmed me in the darkness. I just hated Pete with a passion. Then, morning would come and I would feel like, Okay, people get through worse, we have the virus, we will just take this one thing at a time. I can't torch everything and have the virus at the same time.

I never found out when Pete started up with The Her. In the bits and pieces of time that we got to talk, Pete's accounting of the affair began when he said it became physical. "That doesn't include," I told him, outraged, "the time you were spending with her before you crossed that line." He was mute, maddeningly mute. Pete told me the woman was in hedge funds, also married, with no children. Her name was Sonja and she was German and blond; they had met at a cocktail party after work. Iris had been three at the time. Sonja went back and forth to Berlin, where her husband lived. It was intermittent, which somehow, in Pete's mind, made it less of a big thing. "It's not like I saw her every day, every weekend; it's not like this was a constant thing, Alice," he said. Which made no difference to me, and I said that. On the internet, I found images of Sonja, who was tall and leggy and elegant. I imagined that, God, they were probably even sexting, something I, myself, had never done or even considered doing.

When I looked at his phone while he was sleeping, nothing was there. Of course, I knew he could do all kinds of things to hide messages; he was adept. But I couldn't argue that he was physically there, in the apartment, looking like shit.

And then we came to Maine with Ingmar and our books and bottles of water. And Pete was not going anywhere. We didn't have time to talk or fight anything out. We couldn't go to therapy. The kids were with us constantly. There was no space, or time, to fix what had been broken, even if it could be fixed.

When the waterfall happened, something cleared up, though, in my mind, like that fog Pete yelled at me about was finally lifting over the ocean. It's not that in the last five years I hadn't seen how much Pete loved Iris. I had seen it: they got up early together in the mornings on weekends and he played card games with her while he fed her frozen waffles and syrup. But until that moment when Iris almost drowned I had not felt it. I was never sure he loved her enough. Loved any of us *enough*. That night, though I said, "Thank you for saving her."

"I'd save all of you, if I could."

The moon was shining so brightly through the window, it almost seemed like day, I remember that.

"When Iris was a baby, I didn't think you loved her."

"How could I not love our daughter, Alice?"

"Because you're a fucking asshole, Pete."

"I was exhausted. And I was scared too. And then she was difficult. More than difficult."

"You told her one night—I heard you—that no one would ever love her if she was the way she was, which was the way she was."

"I said what?"

"You told her one night that no one was ever going to love her. You don't even remember that, do you?"

The longest pause in the world. And then, "Actually I do. I felt horrible after I said it. How did you even hear me?"

"I was on my way to the bathroom. You were bouncing her on that plastic ball we had."

"Alice." He turned to me, his face open and pleading. "Jesus, you have been holding on to this all these years? I could have explained. I was angry and panicking and exhausted and you and I weren't talking and I was afraid that she was going to be the kind of person who made everything hard, relentlessly hard. I was worried I wouldn't love her. I was scared I might not love my own daughter, Alice. I wasn't sure I could handle her; I felt undone by how difficult she was. It was a stupid thing to say. After I said it, I told her I was sorry. I'm guessing you didn't hear that part." Suddenly he sounded choked up. I remember looking not at his face, but at one of his arms, the way his hand was leaning into the bed, and the way his fingers were grabbing the sheets, his knuckles tense, the dark hair up his arm.

I knew I should express empathy. I knew I could choose to acknowledge the long years I was not at all interested in anything to do with him while I tried to survive the intensity of Iris, not to mention my anger that I'd never written a second play, my grief that the theater world, which felt so right and homey to me, had been carried away, sailed out of sight, beyond the horizon. But where empathy could have been formed into words, instead my mouth felt like a wide-open prairie in Nebraska where a cold, dry wind was scraping over the land, until every blade of grass was bent into submission. Pete watched me struggle with silence and then, mercifully, he only nodded and lowered his head.

After the waterfall, Iris went back to having sleeping troubles again. Every night, she climbed like a little chipmunk up the bed between us and nestled in, wriggling her little body into the safe place between us. As suddenly as our sex life had briefly bloomed, it withered. Some nights, I got up and went into Iris's bed in the early morning light to sleep alone, away from the wiggly movements of Iris and Pete snoring into his pillow.

As summer wore hotly on, and Iris's presence in the bed seemed unending, Pete asked me tentatively if I thought Iris could be trained to sleep in her own bed at the age of five. I could tell Pete wanted to be alone again in the bed; our sex had been incandescent for those short, hot, damp weeks of July. But for me, being that close physically had opened some hidden faucet inside me: I found myself weeping while doing things like laundry during the day or buttering the girls' toast. I could see that Pete was hoping that perhaps our meetings in the middle of the mattress late at night meant we were beginning a kind of healing. He wanted more. Though he never said any of these things.

I am the broken one, I kept thinking. There is something wrong with me that I cannot get over this. In therapy in the field, I would cry when I saw Lois's face appear on the screen.

"I'm so angry all the time," I told her. "I'm like Sandra Bullock in that movie. Everything about the last few years—Trump and Brett Kavanaugh and #MeToo and George Floyd and Pete and this whole disgusting system of racism and sexism and there's no space anywhere, ever. Everyone's on top of each other, stinking up the bathroom, dirtying dishes. And then the other night as Sophie and I watched *Hamilton* I felt like the biggest fucking failure in the world. He's only forty! I could have done so much more with my life . . . with my work . . . more than dishes and picking up toys."

"Tell me more," said Lois.

And then I told Lois about a friend named Lori who had emailed me and told me she was leaving her husband. Lori wanted to know if our apartment was free. By the time I wrote back and said, "Of course," Lori had found another place. But what irked me was how Lori had said that she wanted to give her kids an experience of "what a good marriage looked like." That phrase got under my skin, intensified the feeling that nothing I had done in my life was right, that I wasn't teaching my girls a good marriage, and this was yet another failure.

"Ah, the good marriage," Lois said. "What do you imagine when you say those words?"

"I don't know," I said. "I think I see lots of smiling and I don't see such hard work. I see something easier. I don't see myself angry all the time, I see myself happy."

"When is the last time you remember being happy, Alice?"

"A few weeks ago I was happy. Actually, I am sometimes happy here, in Maine. With no one going anywhere. With us all sealed in. It's not when Pete is happy. Like during or after sex. It's in a quiet moment, or when we're playing a board game, or eating eggs. It's when I feel like we are a family, and we love each other."

"It feels safe to you?"

"It does."

"And that makes you happy?"

"Yes. Happier."

"What would happen if you let yourself feel safe and also happy, and you decided to stop trying to decide right now about your marriage? We've all been given a chance to hit pause on our lives. A get-out-of-jail-free card. Forget your friend Lori and her decision to divorce in the middle of Covid. For all we know she's being irrational. Try to just be in your life, Alice. With Pete and your girls and in Maine. Love your life. Forget everything that happened before Covid. If this is 'your one wild and precious life,' now is the moment to enjoy this adventure of Maine and the water and the sky and the fact that you all are together and healthy and you still love this man, and even more, you love those girls."

* * *

Days and weeks passed and then it was the end of August.

One night, Pete came into our bedroom from working after dinner. The windows were all open and we could hear crickets and the ocean smelled beautifully salty. I was in bed reading *The New Yorker* with a clip-on reading light, a new story by an Indian author about an adopted child. Iris was sleeping soundly beside me, her little quieted mouth hanging vulnerably open.

Pete sat down. "We need to talk about school, Alice. About New York. About going back."

"I've already said I'm not going back."

"But the girls. Their school. Friends. They fight nonstop here. I've paid tuition. We need to move them back to their lives."

"No."

"That's it?"

"That's it."

"What are you becoming, some kind of unschooler? What about their social lives?"

"You can go back, Pete. But we are not. A year in Maine will not kill either one of them. They can read books. I'm not going back to New York."

"The money, Alice."

"Fuck the money. Our whole lives have revolved around money. Not this time. This is too big, and, I am sure, for once in my life, I am *sure* about something. And that is that we stay here. In Maine."

"You're raising your voice. Iris—"

"Pete." Everything that had not been discussed since March was suddenly pouring out of me like hot lava, shocking me with its intensity. "Don't you ever tell me what to do. You have nothing to stand on. Go if you want. If you go, you do not come back. Go back to The Her, go back to our lives, you do it. But you will not come back here. We can't take the risk, and beyond that, I'm not going back to those lies. I will never go back to our apartment, our bedroom."

"Alice—"

"Do not cut me off—"

"Alice—!" Pete raised his voice now.

"Mommy?"

"Yes, honey. Go back to sleep. Daddy and I were just talking. Everything is fine."

"Is Daddy yelling?"

"No, no."

Pete stood helpless. "I'm right here, Pickle. You are safe. Daddy will be in soon."

He stood staring at me. I clicked off my light so I couldn't see his face. When he had finally left the room, I turned the light back on and finished the story. Then I lay down and tried to sleep.

Later, in the dark, I saw him come in and undress. He got into bed.

In a quiet voice, he volleyed my name over Iris's body. "Alice?"

"Yes."

"Okay. We'll do it your way. We will stay. As long as we can.

One day they will ask me to come back to work. And when they do, we will have no choice."

"*I* will have a choice, Pete."

"Then I may not."

"That's right."

Silence. *Breathing of statues.*

"I'm sorry for all of it. I hope you will forgive me. If not now, then someday. I want you to forgive me. I want to make it right."

I was silent. The night was so dark, the moon so perfectly round. And then this weird, warm rush came over me. I felt, I think it was, forgiveness. It was almost like I was peeing my pants in my sleep. I'd had no idea that forgiveness could be a physical feeling, that the brain could lag behind the body. I had always thought it was an intellectual concept. But it felt so warm and good, like I was deep inside a dream, and my body just let go. I didn't want to share it with Pete quite yet. "I'll tell him tomorrow," I told myself. "That way I can make sure this is real, see if it stays."

And then the cool August night was upon us and outside the crickets sang their farewell songs, and I felt, for the first time in years, maybe, indescribably, undeniably, incredibly hopeful.

# 9

• • •

# Indian Summer

When I wake up I'm not so sure anymore. Forgiveness is a fleeting thing. Here in the darkness of night, gone in the clear blue sky of morning. I seem to be constantly holding this scale in my hand bearing the two ideas: move on and love; stay angry and leave. Am I strong enough to get through this? Would it make me stronger to leave? Maybe Fitzgerald would have said that this is my mark of true genius, this ability of mine to hold two opposing ideas at once. To me it feels like torture. This lack of commitment to any which direction.

I've joined a new online group on Zoom. Tuesday nights a bunch of white women from the girls' school back home meet to talk about systemic racism and what to do about it. There is a lot of wringing of hands and people saying "I don't know" and "like" into the Zoom cameras. Where to start is the problem. Everyone's afraid to say the wrong thing, so we light on trivial matters and stay there. Someone had gotten a haircut the other day, and we all admired it, hungry for haircuts. I sit outside on our terrace to get out of the way of the pre-bedtime insanity. Pete always gets Iris more worked up by wrestling with her and pretending she's his pillow and he's fallen asleep. The girls scream and laugh and I kind of hate it. But I'm outside on the computer, talking to other grown-ups about real-world problems and this drops me back into perspective: how fortunate we are! When I forget, I think Covid has leveled the playing field for all of us; then I remember that I have a second house, a husband making a pile, I'm not Black. I can afford to not know and not know and not know and not know.

When I leave the meetings, after Pete has put the girls to bed, he says, "You staging a coup?"

"Fuck off," I say.

Pete laughs when I say that.

I was remembering this lately: when I was about Sophie's age, my dad took me to the Minnesota Zoo. I have a photo from that day framed and hanging on the hall wall between the kitchen and the bathroom back in our apartment in New York: I am blond, with crisp bangs across my forehead and barrettes on either side. I am wearing blue-and-white checked shorts and a T-shirt that says *Twins* across the front in cursive, and I am sitting on a camel and my dad is standing next to me wearing chinos and holding a cigarette pinched between his thumb and first finger.

I don't think he had moved back home yet when we went to

the zoo that day. I remember this was a deliberate thing: outing with me, alone. Outing with Brian, alone. Brian got a baseball game. I got the zoo.

A couple of weeks later, when he finally did move back in, I remember the feeling of relief. My mother had been erratic and short-fused with him gone. The mornings before school had been chaos: a hodgepodge of cereal from the ends of several mashed bags and a search for socks in an ever-growing tower of laundry. She no longer went in to work, but she didn't clean our house either. I have no idea what she did all day. She was distant, and it was hard to tell where I stood with her, or if she even saw me. When Daddy was home, things felt all right, even if the silence between them loomed like a creature.

Last night Pete and I had a fight. I am shocked sometimes by how raw my anger is, how it unfolds right in front of the kids, how as soon as they turn their backs I give him the finger. How he gives it right back. Sometimes I bare my teeth!

The weather is hot and dry. The field gives off an intense grassy smell as it bakes in the hot sun, and it vibrates during the day with cicadas and by night with crickets. Black-eyed Susans stretch from the driveway to the edge of the woods, like the famous van Gogh painting of sunflowers. In the evenings, the sky is a deep blue and the ocean mirrors it. On the way to the fish market the other day, Sophie told Pete she hated it here. This is what Pete told me. That she was done with "hanging out." That it was September and she wanted to go back to school; she wanted her friends.

That night after she went to bed, he yelled at me. We'd been drinking wine, which at first always seems like a good idea, like we'll laugh and things will ease a bit, but later, it unleashes demons. "You extracted that from her," I said. "She's been happy."

"Alice, don't be pathetic. How can this extended time in Maine be good for her? Kids need school. She needs friends."

"And what did you tell her?"

"I told her I agreed. That I thought she should be in school too. That I would talk to you."

"Great job, Pete. I am the one who's standing in the way?"

"Wait. That's not what I meant."

"Pete, don't bullshit me. She's fine. She's reading. We hike all over. She's outside. We talk about books."

"She's not fine."

"I've tried teaching both of them. I ordered all those workbooks and colored pencils. They just want to be outside. It's just a few months of their lives. It's *fine*. I know that in my heart."

"I think they need more. Sophie needs more."

"You figure it out."

"What I've figured out is that we go back to the city and take our chances with Covid."

"Ha! You have your own reasons for going back. I'm not going. Plus, what would we do differently? She'd sit inside our apartment and do school online. Have you forgotten that part? She can do that here. But she refuses."

"Okay. There's a school here. There are schools—plural—here. I drive by them all the time. Kids are there. I see the kids, Alice."

"And I see lots of people driving around with New York and

Massachusetts plates. There are lots of kids and families still here. It's not just us."

"We don't know what they're doing. Who they are. They might all be eighty, for all we know."

"Whatever. You take this on, Pete. You call schools and find out how to get our kids in and what is needed. I do everything around here. I'm exhausted from mothering and cooking and picking up the house while you work in the office all day and most of the night. I'm exhausted from being the one who thinks ahead and then not even having anything to think ahead to right now, except the same stuff tomorrow and tomorrow and tomorrow. Lately, I can't even think ahead to tomorrow, if that makes any sense. So, yes, you do that. If that's what they need, good. This is an evolving situation."

"Fine."

Later at night, Pete came and stood in the doorway while I was reading in bed. "I have a thought," he offered, and came and sat on the bed next to my legs. "If the kids were not here all day, what would you do?"

I thought for a moment. I knew this was an olive branch. It was almost inconceivable, thinking about the kids not being around, underfoot.

"You know what I miss most about my life?" I asked, my eyes suddenly burning with the clarity of what I was about to say. "I've been thinking about it since we've been here. I miss being in a theater. I miss seeing my words take shape inside actors. I miss working with other people. Like you work with other people. Heck, I even miss waitressing right now. I didn't know how much I missed it all until we came here, until this all happened. In New York, there were so many people everywhere I didn't know I missed anything, or I didn't have time to miss my life. Like I do now."

"I miss people too. Do you remember right before you had Sophie and you were workshopping an early draft of that play you were working on? And you were working with that actor in some black box we'd rented and you invited that director dad from Sophie's school, Adam Schwartz, to come watch?"

"Oh, God, that was awful. He was friends with the actor—the guy with the gaping, bearded smile: Mark."

"And wasn't Adam just a fucking asshole?"

"He was *such* an asshole. He took over my rehearsal and started rewriting my script. He was saying things like 'I think it would work better if it said this. Try that, Mark. That gets to the meaning better.' He was the worst of all that male theater bullshit. Do you remember how, later, he saw me at school and told me he'd written a part for Mark into that new movie of his, and he'd based it on the character in my play? He said it like it was an honor he was bestowing. God, what a creep."

"I remember you kind of stalled big-time on the play after that."

"Well, no. I had Sophie. And it just got away from me. And—well, it's been years now."

"I think you should get back to it. I was thinking that weeks ago when we watched that play online, the one about the family that goes to their upstate house and the guy gets Covid. You could have written that. Better than that."

"When? I feel like I have no time."

"I think we can find the time if we send the kids to school."

"Okay."

"Okay?"

"Thank you. Yes. You call."

"I want the old you back, Alice," Pete whispered and reached out and touched the side of my face.

"Ha. I don't know if that person exists anymore, Pete." I felt myself harden with the shock that that might actually be true, that so much about me and who I was is changed, and the me that was once inside me might be gone forever. And so it goes, tennis: ball over the net, then whacked back.

* * *

The next day, Sophie woke up late. She came out dressed in her Harry Potter robe, holding a wand she had whittled in August out of a branch from the oak that Dale & Co. took down in March. Just as I was stepping outside to go to the garden, she startled me by yelling, "Avada Kedavra."

"Eek." I played along.

"You need to drop down and die, Mom," she said, deadpan.

"Oh, right. I forgot." I crumpled to the floor and splayed my legs out and left my mouth hanging agape.

"You're dumb," she said, a smile twitching along the edges of her lovely, smooth, oh-so-pink lips.

"Let me hug you." I got up and squeezed her and said, "Now go conjure up some breakfast. There's some French toast on the sideboard, and strawberries. I'm going out to the garden."

Pete was in the kitchen talking to a school in Blue Hill. I could hear his voice following me as I closed the screen door, walked across the porch and then down, in my bare feet, to the cold slate terrace. I could tell by his "Hmm-hmm" that he was scratching something down on paper, and that they were likely offering to give us a tour later that week.

I went to work shifting the girls' pumpkins ever so slightly toward the sun so they would turn orange. I heard Sophie screech and the screen door bang, then running bare feet.

She was standing before me, her face on the verge of tears, her wand hanging limply from her hand.

"Oh, Pumpkin," I said. Pete was coming out behind her, his face set.

I held her to me and she started to cry.

"I can't go to a new school," she heaved.

"Would you like to go online today and see your friends? Try it out again?"

"No. I hate online school. I don't want to see anyone like that. I want this to be over."

Oh, my sweet girl. To be eleven now, with so little history of the "before." How would it not feel like this was the new forever? "I know. This is just horrible. This is just such a hard time in your young life. Daddy wants you to be happy. To feel good. He's just worried."

Pete stepped closer and rubbed her back. He said, "This is a hell of a time to be a kid." Tentatively, she leaned her side into him the way his dog, Finn, used to lean into him. He pulled her ever so slightly toward him so he could get his arm around her. I saw love and safety ripple through her body in the way that only a dad can give his daughter.

I felt myself noticing that her breasts were becoming bigger and pointier. We probably needed a bra soon; those little camisoles I had bought her last spring would no longer suffice. I could order one from Amazon and see if she liked wearing it. I'd have to be careful, make sure I was delicate about it. On top of everything else, she was navigating burgeoning puberty up here in Maine with none of her friends to talk to as it happens, to share tales of pads and Tampax attempts and bloody underwear. I remember my friend Jen and I both got our periods the same summer and we'd show each other our bloody pads; they were badges of honor hiding fear of what was to come, what we did not know.

"I know how hard this is, sweetie. You must be so tired of having only Iris to play with and us to talk to," Pete was saying into her hair. "Here's an idea: How about we think of a project you are willing to do, something we can do together. Something you can learn from. It can be anything. Anything at all. Tell me tonight at dinner. Then we can stay up and plan it out together? Sound okay?"

Sophie nodded and leaned deeper into his chest.

"I know what I want to do," she said softly.

Iris reappeared just then from behind the barn. Her knees were caked in dirt and grass like she'd been digging with the spades of her sharp knees.

"Runty's missing," she announced.

"I'm sure he's there. He's just hiding," I said.

"Iris, you're annoying. Go away," said Sophie.

"Ooh, is big baby sister crying?"

"Shut up, Iris."

"Iris, want to help me pick beans?" I took her hand. "We need to find enough for dinner tonight."

"Baby's a crybaby," she taunted.

"Iris, cut it out," I told her. "Come with me."

"No. I don't wanna pick the beans."

"Okay, let's go down to the water. Go get your bathing suit."

"Yippee. I'm going to the water, Sophie, and you aren't." She stuck out her tongue at her sister.

"You can come too, Sophs," I said.

"I hate her," Sophie growled.

"Just come. I'll get your suit. You can change in the barn. Daddy needs to get back to work."

"Later, will you let me hear about your idea?" Pete said. Together we left Sophie in the garden and walked back to the house.

"Thank you," I said to Pete.

"We have to start somewhere," he said. For a moment we were united; we were parenting. It felt so grown-up.

After dinner, while I put Iris to bed, I could hear Sophie chattering to Pete. She was telling him she wanted to make a film, something true, maybe a documentary.

"What about, Cupcake?" Pete asked.

"About Maine? Something here? Our life? Maybe the field and all the bugs? Something real?"

Her voice was all optimism. When Sophie is happy, it seems like the whole house is happy. She is the barometer of how well we are doing. Everyone's muscles relax onto their skeletons when she is fine. When she is not fine, I feel like a failure. "First child thing," Lois says. "There's all this guilt around the first kid. First kids can become like oracles, rather than just kids."

A week later, boxes arrived.

"What is all this stuff?" I asked Pete as he schlepped them all into the living room.

"It's for Sophie's movie," he said. "Sophs, let's open the boxes. Come on, Iris, you can pop the bubbles in the bubble wrap." Sophie stood to the side, behind one of the couches, taking the tower of boxes in. Pete started opening them and revealed, with the enthusiasm of a game-show host, a digital camera, cords, a light meter, a tripod, clamps, color cards, some kind of black box, rechargeable batteries and their charger, and studio lights. As he pulled them out, he showed each new thing to Sophie, exclaiming about how shiny and cool it all was. Packing peanuts and bubble wrap were strewn all over the floor. His face was lit up, like a kid on Christmas. He started fiddling immediately with the camera while Sophie watched. "Sophs, you stoked?" he asked.

A shadow passed over my daughter's face. Listlessly she said, "Yeah." And looked at the floor.

"Sophie Anne," Pete began, an edge to his voice. "I just got you all this nice gear. Let's make a movie! This is what the professionals use!"

"I didn't want all this stuff. This is too much. This is for someone who knows what they're doing. All I wanted was to try."

"You'll learn. We can make it fun."

"I don't want it. I wanted a camera."

"You got a camera!"

"That's a huge heavy thing. I don't want that. I wanted something small that I could carry around."

"I got you a case!" He held up a blue nylon padded bag.

"That case is stupid. I'll look like an idiot carrying that."

Pete looked crestfallen and then grumpy. "It's the kind of case a real photographer carries. Sophie, this is what you wanted." He was trying hard not to lose his temper.

"No, it's what you wanted. I don't want it. You probably spent a million dollars on all this." She plopped herself down on the couch, her face firm and intractable.

"Don't you want to make your movie?" he asked.

"No, I really don't. Not anymore. Nope!" Her lips smacked annoyingly.

From the kitchen I started motioning to Pete to shut up. I was waving my arms and mouthing, "Let. It. Go."

"Fine," he said angrily, shooting me a glance. He began packing everything back up. In a huff, he took all the boxes out to the barn and then went into his office and shut the door.

Sophie looked at me. Her chin started to quiver.

"I didn't want all that stuff," she whimpered when I came and sat down and put my hand on her knee. "It's too much. It's like he does this stuff for himself."

"He was just excited. He wanted to go *all in* for you and with you. You know how Daddy gets. He's not exactly a subtle guy."

"I feel like he doesn't listen."

"He listens. He just wants to give you the moon and the stars."

"It's too much pressure. He can't ever just be low-key. It's so embarrassing."

"Sophie. Daddy loves you. That much I know." She was done with this conversation. Her hands were playing with her earbuds. "Okay, listen to your music. I'll work on dishes. It will be okay."

Later, when I was checking on Iris, I heard Pete ask Sophie to walk down to the water with him. I heard her assent. I heard the screen door squeak and then Pete close it firmly so Ingmar couldn't get out. I heard them laughing as they walked away from the house.

I was remembering when Sophie was about two or three and Pete was traveling a lot. And how Sophie and I would get into our own rhythm and then he'd come back and it would be awkward for a day or so, and Sophie would be more attached to me than to him. But then how she'd warm and the two of them would do everything together. He always made her laugh back then. It must be weird for him not knowing how to make her laugh anymore.

My own dad made me laugh in a way no one else ever could. When he came home that summer many, many years ago now, it was hard not to forgive him. Time just closed back over. For me, anyway. I never really thought about it until later, but I'm not sure I heard him and my mother laugh much anymore together. But he did laugh with Brian and me: roughhousing in the leaf piles outside, playing touch football on Thanksgiving, being silly at dinner.

Being a family is like that, I thought. We're always coming in and then going back out like the tide. The real question is, can you bear the mud flats in between?

# 10

• • •

# Lost

Later Pete would tell Alice that it was Iris who realized first.

It was late afternoon but already the sky was a deep blue against the dark forms of the pointed firs. The last vestiges of light glowed yellow behind that massive swath of blue and illumed the flaming fauve trees. The barn stood gray and silent, and for a moment longer its clapboard trimmed peak shone a brilliant white pointing into the sky, and then fell into dusky shadow. If you were outside looking in, the lights lit up the little house in orange squares and you might hear the chatter of two girls and their father. And then you would have heard Iris scream, "Daddy," and some other words after that, and then seen from the outside the scampering of three forms around the house. And then the old oak door opened and the screen door banged open and closed after that and then the breath of a human puff into the cold air and then Pete pulling on boots and a coat, and then switching on a flashlight. Iris bursting out the door just after her father, and then Sophie in a T-shirt. You'd have heard Iris yell, "Innnnngmaaar!"

Alice had gone to Ellsworth, triple masked—N95, medical, and then cloth—to get cat food and litter at Walmart and to food shop and get the oil changed in their car. Her errands were stretching into the early fall gloaming. Pete was on his own with the girls for the first long stretch of time since the pandemic began. And somehow, at some point, who knows when, Ingmar had gotten out on his watch.

Pete banged a tuna fish can and Sophie held a bag of food and was shaking it. Sophie went around one side of the house, while Pete, with Iris clutching the end of his shirt, went around the other, calling. Every so often, Pete leaned down to peer with his flashlight under the porch and into the dark gaps under the barn. He continued slowly, methodically, calling. Iris was already crying and imagining the worst, as she tended to do, and swinging her flashlight all over the place, making it confusing. Every so often from the other side of the house you could hear Sophie hiss, "Iris, stop warbling. I can't hear anything if you warble." Which only made Iris warble more.

Soon, the trio was on their way to the woods, calling and banging. Pete asked each girl when they had last seen the cat. "Today," said Iris. "In the morning. I was making him that toy with my old sock and he was chasing it."

"What time was that?" asked Pete, realizing that this was an absurd question to ask his five-year-old.

"I said. The morning," said Iris.

"Sophie?" asked Pete.

"Uh. I dunno. I think I saw him in the afternoon, maybe? It all blends together."

"Okay, he can't have been gone long," Pete hoped.

As they got closer to the woods, Pete seemed to lose his nerve. The white pines loomed large in the dark before them.

"Sophie, go back inside," Pete barked. "Go look in every possible place you can think of—inside the laundry hamper in the hall, on top of the towels in the bathroom, under the couch, in the pantry, on Iris's bed. Anywhere. And while you're at it, get a coat—it's terrifically cold out here."

"Terrifically cold," answered Sophie, her sass unmistakable. And off she went. Sophie, of course, was old enough to remember another time Ingmar was lost, but only in the hallway in New York. In the chaos of her little sister's birth it had been a huge drama, and her mother had been furious at her father, even though Sophie was quite sure it had been their grandmother who had forgotten to close the door. It was little things like that that Grannie did that Sophie tried to help with: leaving the door open, piling the dishes all over the place, never remembering where to put the teacups or her lunch box, folding all the laundry into the wrong piles. Sophie knew it irritated her mother, but Sophie found it amusing and sort of like a game. "Oh, Grannie," she said. "Silly, this is Mama's underwear, not mine."

"So it is, dear," her grandmother said, appraising the large lavender-colored pair of her mother's underwear. And Sophie would run it into her mother's room and put it away in the little drawer that smelled of rose petals, while her grandmother piled the soft bath towels on the shelf in the closet next to the girls' bathroom.

"Daddy, will we find Ingmar?" Iris wanted to know.

"Yes," said Pete, setting his jaw. For a second he let his mind wander to the question, "What if we don't?" The idea made him feel nauseous. It would be a failure of incredible magnitude. Of his. So instead he said, "Of course we will."

When he and Iris got to the woods, which Sophie had renamed the Forbidden Forest, they stood for a moment on the edge peering into the darkness. In there, the last vestiges of blue no longer reached and it was *dark* dark.

"I can't imagine he's in here," said Pete and banged his tuna fish can. "Let's turn back. I'm not convinced he'd have gone this far. Ing is a city cat. Scared of his own shadow."

"Daddy, remember the time Ing didn't even know what to do with the mouse in the kitchen?"

Pete chuckled, trying to sound good-natured, light. "Exactly," he said.

As they turned back, Sophie reappeared and said she hadn't found Ingmar anywhere inside. The three of them trudged with their flashlights back across the field, calling. They circled the barn once again and went down the driveway. And then they began the onerous task of going out to the road and looking there for a body. Though that's not what Pete said. He said,

"Let's see if Ing could be here in the bushes along the side of the road, or down near the skunk cabbages."

Nothing. Cars passed them every so often, slowing down.

"You know the green house on the rise over the stream?" Sophie eventually asked. "Can we go ask there?"

"He'd never have gone that far," Pete snapped.

"How do we know? We don't even know them. They don't even know we have a cat," countered Sophie.

"Please, Daddy," piped up Iris.

"Okay, we can try. But your mother will be home soon," Pete said.

They trudged down the road toward their nearest neighbor, who lived in the putty-green raised ranch on a small piece of scrubby land. In the daylight, when they drove past, Pete had seen a truck out front on cinder blocks, a basketball hoop, and various wheelbarrows and lawnmowers peeking out from under a blue tarp that was weighted down on one side with bricks. A brown Honda CR-V sat in the drive. In the yard were a row of six orange Home Depot buckets filled with dirt and now-dead tomato plants, a faded plastic Christmas reindeer lying on its side, and a pile of wood ready for winter, cleanly stacked against a shed; on the other side of the shed, a dozen or so old lobster traps were piled.

As they climbed the driveway, his two daughters quietly swinging their flashlights next to him, Pete felt a twinge of anxiety that this would be awkward, that they were strangers in a strange land that they pretended wasn't a strange land and yet was. And then Pete remembered a time when he and Alice went to Paris, before they were married. They had spent five days there, eating croissants and going to the Louvre and Rodin's sculpture garden, having lavish multicourse dinners in little bistros and then walking along the Seine in the dark. It was a luxurious and amazing time at the beginning of their relationship. But there had been this one funny moment, Pete remembered, when they were in the Marais and had gone into a little shop full of trinkets and curios—old clocks a million years old, watches on chains, and military medals once awarded to someone no longer stomping around this mortal coil. The shop had been full of cats, and, way in the back, was an old woman with a shawl polishing a candlestick. He and Alice had been quietly looking at all the shiny little things when the woman appeared from the back, clutching her shawl about her, her glasses low on her nose. She had spoken sharply to them in French. It seemed she didn't like them picking things up and touching them and looking at them, or maybe she thought they were going to steal something? That couldn't have been it. Though Alice spoke a little French, this woman spoke quickly and with an accent Alice couldn't quite place, perhaps it had a tinge of Russian or Hungarian. But the woman was irritated or distressed by something that neither he nor Alice was able to discern. She seemed to be telling them to get out of the store, which alarmed them. Back out on the street, he and Alice had laughed, but Pete still remembered that odd feeling he had, that they were not welcome somewhere, or that they were behaving badly without knowing it, that just by their mere existence they had been out of step. He always wondered if there was something else the woman was trying to tell them, like she needed help, or a cat had gotten out, and he wondered if the woman had been shocked when they started laughing and left the store.

When Pete and Iris and Sophie got to the steps of the ranch, Pete told the girls to stand back, as no one was masked. He went to the door and knocked.

After some shuffling inside, the door opened and an old man opened the door, pulling an oxygen tank behind him on wheels that fed small plastic tubes into his nose. He wore a pair of chocolate-colored corduroys that were rubbed smooth at the knees and a red flannel shirt and green fleece vest. He had small glasses and his nose was red-veined. On his feet were some scuffed blue slippers.

"Excuse me," said Pete. "I'm your neighbor," and he pointed behind him at their house through the trees and over the field.

The man nodded and wheezed, then inhaled sharply through his tubes, his nostrils dilating. "Ayuh," he said, as if it were a fact he already knew.

"And we lost our cat. He's big and black. Green eyes. My daughters . . ." Pete's voice trailed off and he turned his body to show the man his children. "They are worried and want their cat back . . . and we were wondering, could you have seen him?"

"Stay right theah," the man said, and shut the door. Through the little diamond-shaped windows cut into the door Pete could see the man shuffle off down the hall with the tubes and the wheels and the blue slippers.

"Where did he go?" asked Sophie.

"No idea," said Pete. "Maybe he's getting his boots."

A little while later, he heard the man shuffling back, and when he opened the door, he was holding Ingmar in one hand and the oxygen tank carrier in the other. Ing's long black body was pressed against the man, his head sort of squished as the man had Ing clutched under the arms. Ing's green eyes were darting about.

"Ingmar," squealed Iris, and forgetting Covid, she ran forward, saying, "Oh, thank you so much, sir, thank you."

The man laughed, then gasped a little and said, "Okay, easy does it. You got 'im? Hold on tight theah."

Iris nodded solemnly and said, "I got him."

Pete said, "Oh my gosh, I never in a million years expected this. Where did you find him?"

The man said, "Juss comin' home from the grocery stoah tonight, saw a black cat on the side a the road. Slowed down and thought he'd run off into them trees, but he sat down. So I pulled ovah and called him and he came right to me. No colla. Figured I'd call the SPCA in the mornin'."

"Thank you, sir. Thank you. I'd shake your hand if we could. We live just over there—if you ever need anything. Thank you." Pete beamed.

"Thank you," said Sophie.

"Good night then," the man said. "Glad you got your cat." And then he shut the door and Pete and the girls heard him shuffle back down the hall, the wheels following his footsteps.

As they turned to walk down the man's driveway, Iris said, "Daddy, how come you never asked his name?"

Pete clapped his hand on his mouth. "Oh my God," he said. "I don't know. I was so focused on Covid distance and Ingmar and you girls . . . I never said mine either. I'm out of practice with people, I guess."

"It's okay, Daddy. We have Ing now."

"Would you like to make the man a thank-you card?"

"Sure. I can do that," said Iris, all optimism and sunshine.

\* \* \*

Years from now, Pete would remember that night, the near miss of it. Being outside in the dark with his girls, the responsibility of his daughters' hearts, which he held, so precious, in his palm. And the kindness of the next-door neighbor, who was, bizarrely, still a stranger. Being part-time, impermanent residents, they still did not know anyone; community was not what they had searched for or fostered when they came to Maine. They had come to isolate in summers, to bring friends from New York, to sail and swim and eat and drink Sauvignon Blanc.

And then he'd remember how Alice's car had swung into the drive, the high beams freezing them all in the driveway, as if they had been caught robbing a 7-Eleven, and how Iris was clutching Ingmar when Alice had stepped out of the car and come from the darkness and into the car lights and said, "Oh my God." Pete remembered seeing her long hair and how white and ovate her face was, her lips so perfectly pink in the bright silos of light, as if painted by Titian. And then how she'd understood and put her arms around Iris, whose face was beaming but crusty around the eyes where there had been tears not so long ago. Alice had held Iris and Ingmar to her and then she'd looked at Pete searchingly, but not angrily, for the first time in so, so long, and then put her arm around Sophie and said, as if it were just the next most natural thing to do, "Get in. Let's drive up. No seat belts! Come on, Ing—wanna ride?" And they had all piled in around cat food and kitty litter and bags of groceries and ridden to the house, and the relief inside that car and gratitude that they were together was such a feeling, such an incredible feeling, one Pete was sure he'd never felt before.

# 11

• • •

# The Hutch

The hutch was worn and brown and enormous. "Towering" was how Pete described it. Pete had gotten Dale to pick it up in his truck and then drop it in our yard. Dale, in his blue Dickies lined with red flannel, a pack of Marlboro Ultra Lights sticking out of his top pocket, along with a Bic pen and a small, wire-bound notebook, offered to help us drag it inside. But Pete told him we could do it, thinking, he told me later, that all that heaving and pushing with all those heavy breaths inside our house would not be advisable. Dale, after all, was not the kind of dude who wears a mask, Pete pointed out.

"Jesus, Pete. He cut our trees down. And now he's on the team that doesn't wear masks? Why do we even hire him?"

"My God, Alice. Back to this. Because other than all that, he's a solid guy. A good guy. Decent in most ways. Anyone can see that."

"I guess."

Overnight, it seemed, all the leaves were off the ash trees at our southeast border, and the world looked totally different. We found a dead woodchuck on the side of the road one morning. "Is it Runty?" Iris asked as Pete got out of the car and pulled the stiff body into our field.

"No, no," I reassured her. "Runty is still under the barn." But truthfully, I hadn't seen Runty in . . . was it days? Weeks? I couldn't remember when.

On Friday, the president went into the hospital with what was probably Covid. They said it was Covid, but who knows with this guy what is what. Pete was working all weekend to manage the economic fallout. I took the girls out of the house on Saturday.

Something I didn't know: Maybe nobody knows this. Well, obviously *somebody* knows this, because I learned it on that Danish show *Borgen* that I've started watching on Netflix in the evenings when the girls fall asleep—their feet dirty from running barefoot and leaves in their hair, even though fall is arriving and I admonish them regularly to put on socks and shoes, hats even. They are, as Pete loves to point out, "beautifully unschooled." He says this to irritate me, because Trump promised that schools would open "beautifully in the fall." Beautifully in the middle of a pandemic? When Pete says it, I laugh. Some of that old irony between us has come back. When he's funny, I want to pull him into me and hold on; I want to stay in the funny as long as I can.

What I learned, though, was that fifty years ago a U.S. military jet crashed in Greenland with four nuclear bombs on board. One of them is still there. A bomb. Sitting on, or in, ice over the fjord. They can't find it. This is the ice that is melting as the planet warms, by the way. Even Pete has been lured from his work to come sit with me to watch *Borgen*, and we have been holding hands. The screen is a refuge. Every night I say the same thing: "I wish she were our leader."

"I'm sure everyone watching it feels that way," says Pete.

"She is *so* no bullshit," I say, wishing I had been more no bullshit in my own life.

The girls and I found the hutch Saturday at a yard sale. We had driven over the bridge to Deer Isle. Despite the cold wind, we stopped at the beach on the side of the causeway to swim in the high, remarkably warm tide. Afterward, wet and cold, we piled into the car and rolled up all the windows against the wind and ate peanut butter and honey sandwiches and drank peppermint tea I'd made from mint I planted that summer. The ocean we had just frolicked in roiled in front of us, blue and white-capped.

Then we did a wide circle back home, away from the blue ocean and fishing docks of Stonington, up the hill, past the white-spired church, through the changing trees, until we came to a long dirt road with signs for a moving sale at the end. A large white house with an enormous, grand front door loomed through the trees, sitting right on the edge of pink granite rocks looking over the ocean to North Haven. In the driveway, there was an elderly woman sitting in a chair, a denim mask over her face, a long white braid down her soft back. A woman I presumed was her caregiver, with thick meaty ankles and a hard look in her eyes, stood nearby. Her mask had a yellow smiley face on it. Various other people were moving things out of the house, mostly masked. Two people in their twenties, a guy and a woman, millennials, as they say, wore no masks and seemed content to come and go with little compunction, helping move things here and there, sometimes pulling their bandannas up over their mouths, sometimes not.

On the paved drive, bureaus, lamps, and tables full of books and all sorts of things spread out, and beyond onto the grassy lawn. Tarps had been laid down and piles of pillows and blankets were placed on the blue plastic. Heavy, dark wooden antiques were given shelter under the garage roof and spindle-backed chairs lined up against the green privet hedge.

I let the girls go off, telling them not to touch anything, only to look.

"Is this all yours?" I asked the woman in the chair.

"Yes," she replied. "My husband died last year and I moved to a retirement community. I have a small apartment. Fred says I need to sell my house now, when people want to move here from the cities—the virus, you know."

"Yes," I said.

"Are those your little girls?"

"Yes."

"I guess there's no more school for the children. They miss their friends?"

"Yes. They do. And they don't. They are free right now . . . it's hard to explain. I'm sorry you have to sell all your things."

"It will all be over soon."

"I hope so," I said, not knowing what she meant by *all*.

"Wow, that wind. Do you feel it? Sarah! Sarah! Can you bring me my shawl?"

Sarah came, breathing heavily behind her mask, a small wet patch appearing in a round little circle, making the smiley face sag a little.

"The hurricane. It's coming. We better get inside."

"No, Grace, that's somewheah down South. Maybe Texas."

Grace turned to me and said, "The birds, all those birds migrating right into it. They fly over the Gulf, you know. Those tiny hummingbirds. When I lived here I would put out more feeders in September to give them enough energy for the flight. Do you have somewhere safe to go tonight to get out of the wind?"

Sarah interjected, "Grace, we ah safe heah in Maine. It's the people down South."

"Oh! Oh! I have deteriorated so much in the last six months. I am not the same. I worry about a hurricane and it's not coming, I guess." She had a pleasant, if pleading, look on her face.

"That's okay," I said.

"I am interested in death, what it will be like." Her eyes misted over.

"I understand," I said. But I didn't understand, and even worse I wanted her to shut up and not say things like that. It made me uncomfortable to talk about death. Her death. I don't even know her!

When my own grandmother died six years before, I went to her house to clean it out with Sophie while Pete stayed back in New York, working. I was hugely pregnant with Iris at the time and my feet were so swollen I could barely fit them into my ever-widening Birkenstocks. My grandmother had nothing fancy, no antiques, save for an old Singer sewing machine on a wooden table, wrought iron and stained oak. It had been my great-grandmother's. I wanted more than anything to bring that heavy, beautiful relic back home to New York, some piece of history from my ancestors on the Plains. Something that would tie me to the quilt-making, sock-darning person I must be somewhere inside. But, overwhelmed and hot and pregnant, I decided it was too difficult to get it home and I sold it for fifty dollars at a yard sale. A few years later, I read the Roald Dahl story "Parson's Pleasure," and I felt almost as foolish as those farmers who were duped into selling an old and valuable Chippendale commode to a con man.

Here, trying hard not to make eye contact with the old woman's wet, seeping eyes above that denim mask, my eyes landed on a big, dark wooden hutch. It was enormous and would never fit in our car. I wasn't even sure it would fit in our house. But I could just see a vase of blue hydrangeas on it in the dining room. Something about its deep shelves and wide cabinets felt like it was the answer to my life right then. Everything I needed to put away, to hide, to collect and shelve in my life could go inside that hutch. All my stacks of receipts and knickknacks and clay birds and candleholders and kids' drawings and magazines I hoped to one day read. The odd dishes I don't know where to put and some of our lovely silver that is piled into the kitchen shelves. All of it could go behind those dark cherry doors and be forgotten.

"When Paul died, he never really left me, you know." The old woman was starting back on death. I was wriggling in my skin. "At night, after Sarah retires, I talk to him. I tell him about the day and we talk about dinner. He never eats enough. He's still too thin. Every morning he falls out of bed again." I could now see tears sliding out from the bottom of her mask.

I wanted to offer comfort to this woman, so obviously in distress over the loss of her husband. But I didn't know her, and I didn't know if she'd accept someone else's touch when there was so much illness in the air. I couldn't even proffer a kind smile with half my face covered.

I said, "You have been through such a hard thing," trying to crinkle the corners of my eyes to show a smile, knowing how lame it sounded. "It sounds like you loved Paul very much."

"Oh, we had a good time. We always laughed together."

"That's nice."

"Are you married?"

"Yes."

"Do you laugh together?"

"Sometimes. When we don't fight." I was trying to make a joke.

"Oh, you must laugh," she said seriously. "Find something funny to talk about. Or do! We used to watch those old Abbott and Costello routines. Paul would laugh and laugh."

"How much do you want for the hutch?" I asked, too abruptly.

"Oh, I don't know." She was shaken back into real time. "Sarah! Sarah!" she called. Sarah was tagging some new things that had come out and been placed on the blue tarp. She didn't notice. Grace put a whistle to her lips and blew on it with all her spittle strength, and Sarah stiffened like a bird dog and then turned. When she was approaching, Grace called, "How much are we asking for the hutch?"

Sarah called as she walked, "Hundred dollahs."

"Will you take a check?" I asked the old woman. I couldn't bring myself to do business with Sarah and the wet smiley face.

"Yes, yes. Of course." She looked around at the hutch. "That was in my sunroom. We kept all our old opera tapes on there and our records underneath. On Sundays Paul and I would sit down with a glass of sherry—well, sherry for me, he had vodka. A small bowl of pretzels and maybe some very cold salmon on toast and we'd listen to the music. That was really very nice. This"—and she waved her arm grandly, if feebly—"was a beautiful house to live in, a beautiful life."

"Yes," I said again. "I imagine so. How old is it?"

"Oh, old, old. Almost as old as I am!"

Sarah narrowed her eyes at me over her mask. "How are you going to fit this hutch in your car?"

"I don't know. Can I come back for it tomorrow? I'll need to ask my husband to ask someone with a truck to get it for us."

"Grace," said Sarah. "Grace, this woman"—Sarah was suddenly shouting, though I didn't understand why, as Grace seemed to hear me just fine in a normal voice—"she is wondering if she can leave it here until tomorrow or maybe even the next day. She needs a truck."

"Leave what?"

"The hutch, Grace. The big one, over there."

Grace turned and motioned her hand dismissively, like it was a bird flapping through the air, about to land. "Oh, just give it to her."

"She's buying it, Grace. She needs to come back. Oh, damn—hold on! Those cats!"

And then away Sarah went after a small black cat that was chasing a tabby.

"Max," she shrieked to one of the millennials. "Your darn cats got out." The young man was skinny and Brooklyn, wearing all black and Frye boots. His bandanna—also black—fell off his face as he loped after the cats, calling, "Osama! Saddam! Comeer!"

Sarah came back. "Sorry," she huffed and then put her hand up to indicate I shouldn't talk for a moment and stepped away from the driveway into the yard to pull her mask down so that she could take several large gulps of air. When she came back, she explained, "Those two over theah—they have been house-sittin' and they have these dahn cats that can't get out. And the cats keep findin' ways to get out. No one's payin' attention . . ."

I was grateful Iris didn't notice. She was too enthralled with a jewelry box full of lots of glittery, long necklaces to shift her focus to two cats that some unmasked hipsters own.

"Did I hear their names right?" I asked, suddenly feeling a shudder. I was thinking of when I first moved to New York and those planes hit; I was thinking of people jumping and fire and I couldn't wrap my head around naming a furry little cat after a terrorist.

"Don't ask me about it," Sarah retorted. "He thinks it's funny namin' his cats that way. It's offensive, I told 'im. He's just another one of these New Yawkahs, comes up heah and just does what he wants. He's the boyfriend. These people! There was no Covid up heah till all these people with theay summah houses all stahted arrivin' in droves. Not even summah anymoah, and the place is still packed. They shoulda just stayed home!"

"Mommy," called Sophie, pulling me away. "Can I have this clock?" She held up an old box clock with roman numerals, all wood with a crank in the back. "And can I have these?" Iris appeared with the entire jewelry box filled with necklaces and rings and old bracelets—all costume jewelry.

I turned back to Sarah. "How much for these and the hutch?" I asked.

"One fifty."

"I have a check. We can come back tomorrow—will someone be here?"

"We'll be heah. We'll be selling things all week long."

Again Grace piped up. "Just give it to her," she told Sarah.

When I handed Sarah the check, she looked at the New York address. She didn't say anything. Neither did I.

\* \* \*

That night Iris went crazy because she said her ears hurt. There was water trapped in them from our swim. I put her in a warm bath and asked her to dunk her head and hold it underwater. She was being totally irrational and crying and she was angry. "Iris, for God's sake, there's just some water from our swim trapped behind some ear wax. Like a bubble. It will get better. Let me Q-tip them out."

"No," she screamed, holding her ear. "It will hurt."

"I can be very gentle," I tried to reassure her.

She splashed me from the bath and said, "You are being so mean."

Suddenly I had no patience for this. "Okay, fine. I'll send Daddy in," I said and walked out.

I could hear him in the bathroom for what seemed like hours. I was sure the water in her bath had gone cold by now. I could hear him making progress and then just when he thought she would let him put the Q-tip in her ear, I heard her retract and screech, "No, Daddy!"

When she came out, she was still crying. "I have an idea," I suggested. "I've been noticing that you are stuffy in the mornings lately. It's just allergies from the leaves and mold this time of year. How about we give you a little Benadryl? It might just clear up your stuffy nose, and that might help, because your nose and your ears are connected by a long tube." I traced my finger over where I thought the sinuses were on her face. "Want to try that?"

She leaned warily into me and nodded. She was asleep in half an hour, snoring from her room at the top of the stairs.

The next morning, the ear wasn't mentioned. It was Sunday.

"Good God," said Pete when the hutch was dropped off by Dale. "Alice, what were you thinking?"

"Look how dark and beautiful the wood is."

"If we can get it through our narrow doors. Jesus, the thing is mammoth. Where are you thinking this will go?"

"In the dining room. I'll put your mother's silver in there. And all that other crap that's currently piled on the kitchen counter and the window ledge."

"Okay. I guess that will work." He looked doubtful.

"Can we at least try?"

Together we each picked up an end and, straining, tried to walk it closer to the front door. We had to put it down every several feet. Pete pulled out his measuring tape. "It should fit through," he said. "But then, how we're going to turn it, I don't know."

"Can we take it apart?" I asked.

"I've looked," he said. "The back is all one piece, made to rest against a wall. Probably banged together inside the house and never moved until movers took it out a few days ago. We just have to try to navigate it through."

Holding the heavier end, Pete tried to steer us through the opening, but it was just a hair too tight to get all the way through the door frame. We backed it out, both of us yelling about dropping it. "I'm going to be Leonard Bast–ed," I shrieked as he tried to stand it up vertically.

"Sophie," Pete thundered. "So. Phie," he yelled again. Sophie arrived from around the house, where she had been reading in the hammock. Irritatingly she was wearing shorts and a T-shirt and was barefoot even though it was windy, threatening rain— and October. "Sophs, we need your help getting this thing in. If we all get it up high enough, we can get it around the molding there and into the hall," Pete told her.

"Okay, fine," she grumbled and threw her book to the ground. It was an anthology of ghost stories she'd had me order from the library. "Mom, get off your phone," she snarled at me.

"Sophie! Pick up that end," Pete barked. "Alice, seriously, forget the news for a second. You bought this thing. It's now or never."

We all heaved and Pete groaned and we tried to maneuver the unwieldy thing though the door. There was a scrape and a crack and Sophie screamed, "We're breaking it! Stop. It won't fit."

We put it down and, heaving, her arm muscles accentuated like beautiful waves under her skin, Sophie furrowed her brow. "You guys are idiots. You didn't even measure anything. I'm not helping you with this." And with a flounce of her ponytail she was off with her book, back in the hammock.

"Can we get it out of the door?" I asked Pete.

"Only with scraping it pretty badly. That top piece is tearing a bit. Let's try to get it inside, into the hall. Maybe we can maneuver it from there. Can you lift on your end?"

With everything I had, I lifted and Pete pulled and there was another deep scraping sound and it was stuck. "Pete, it's stuck in the door!!"

"Try again. Pick it up and push."

We tried but it wasn't budging. Pete was straining, I was pushing.

"We just need to get it off that one little corner of molding," Pete explained, as if I couldn't see it myself. "Dang it all to hell, this thing. We didn't even need it, Alice! Let's switch places and try to get it out of the house. It's getting dark. We can't leave the door open and it stuck in the door all night."

We switched, and finally, with Pete pulling and my pushing from the other end, there was a loud crack and it slid out of the door with a bang and slammed onto the ground and then tipped over with a shudder into a pile of leaves the girls had been playing in all morning. It had a huge crack up its back and it lay in an almost animated posture of prostrate pain: a whale, beached.

"I'll cover it with a tarp," Pete said. "We can figure this out tomorrow."

After, I stood in the shower for a long time and the water felt warm. I couldn't stop weeping. About what? I didn't know. The broken hutch? Ridiculous. About Grace? A woman I didn't even know? About her dead husband and their sweet happy years spent listening to opera and eating canapés?

Still damp, I made stir-fry from one of our many zucchinis the garden had produced, and looked up how to make homemade hoisin sauce, which, despite its spelling, is *not* pronounced like *voisin* in French, but HOY-sin. Wrapping zucchini and onions and warm scrambled egg in the soft tortillas and slathering them with the sauce was a quiet pause, everyone focused on this small, mundane task.

When the girls were in bed, Pete came and found me. I was sizing up a bench covered with stacks of paper—receipts, bills, letters that needed to be responded to, kids' drawings, magazines, all of which I'd wanted to store out of sight and forget about in the hutch. On the radio I could hear the president's voice; he was saying the presidential debate should be held in person, even though, of course, he could be contagious with Covid.

"I got an email today, Alice. I have to go back to work. In person, at least for a little bit."

"Okay," I said, my stomach immediately clenching. I looked up at him, then looked away. That terrible day I flew at Pete and he left came tumbling back into my mind. I picked up my phone and started refreshing the news, falling through the looking glass into a digital device, something I tell my children not to do. But each time I scrolled, I was rewarded with more external chaos: the president's doctor is a liar; the president wants out of the hospital; this evening he was driving around in an SUV with two Secret Service agents even though he has Covid; Biden and Pence keep campaigning; the president says he's fine; the president says Covid is no big deal.

I heard Pete over the barrage of words on the *New York Times* site. "Alice, the markets have been thrashing around. Wall Street is booming. I can't do as much as I need to do from here. I need to take a few meetings and address some staffing issues. I need to take stock. I told them I'd try to go back and forth. I'll be in my office with the door closed. I can do it safely. The point is, I need to show up."

I looked up at him from the turmoil on the phone, my eyes

squinting through the white light of the screen or maybe it was the conversation, I couldn't tell. "We're not going."

"I know. I haven't asked you to."

"I will need the car."

"I know. I can buy a second car."

"I don't know how you will come back to us."

"We'll figure that out."

"Are you going to see The Her?"

"I've told you, that is over."

"You will go back to The Her. Without Covid, you would have kept seeing her."

"I've told you this before. I was ending it anyway."

"How can I possibly believe you?"

"Alice. Everything is upside down."

"I know. I—"

"Alice, I want you to believe me. I want our family."

"Yes. I believe that." I felt exhausted; I had no more fight. I remembered that I had forgiven him, at least I thought I had. Why did forgiveness seem to wax and wane with the moon? Outside, an apple tree scraped at the window like a witch's finger.

Pete asked, "Who will tell the girls?"

"We will. Together."

"When?"

"Tomorrow morning. That you are going back to work."

"Okay."

"I feel scared, Pete."

"I know."

"We will be divided."

"We don't have to be—"

"Come here," I said. And I held his strong back and pulled him to me and I felt him shudder a bit. "Me too," he whispered into my ear. I didn't look to see if there were tears, but I could feel in the way his back folded and he leaned in that he was as good as crying.

Then he said, "I need you to want this enough to believe in me. That I can change. For our family."

"I'm trying. I'm still just really fucking angry. I don't trust you. You lied to me."

"I'm sorry. I will make it up to you."

Silence.

"Do you love me, Pete?"

"Yes, I love you."

"Why? Why do you love me? Because I haven't always felt it. Like, the way I want to or need to feel it."

"I love you because you're grounded and I'm not. I love you because you're not afraid to get dirty. And at the end of the night, when your hair is wet from your shower, you make my heart thump. The other thing had nothing to do with not loving you."

"It should have had everything to do with loving me."

"I understand."

After a second of silence he asked, "May I kiss you?"

And then our bodies came together in the way they always knew how to, even when we seemed light-years apart.

\* \* \*

The next morning, together, we moved the hutch into the barn. It didn't stand straight anymore, so we had to lean it against the wall and prop it up with some old broken chairs and two cinder blocks so it wouldn't come crashing down on anyone. Who knew what would happen to it. It might sit there a hundred years for all I know, long after we are gone, long after the barn itself collapses. Over the phone, Pete bought a new Subaru wagon and had it delivered to us, for an extra fee. It's silver and the inside is black leather; the girls squealed at the fun of trying out all the new buttons and lights. It has temporary Maine plates, making us legit.

In a few days everything that was fixed and unfixed will lie on the cutting-room floor and Pete and I will now be separated. Winter is coming, I can smell it in the wind. The impractical practicality of our house in winter niggles around the edges of my stunned realization that the girls and I will be on our own, at least for a while. For years I have wanted to leave Pete. But now, as his departure is imminent and I have no idea if I can trust him back in New York, I feel some of the ice inside my heart that melted over the summer start to freeze up again. I'm not sure we've found all our warheads and chipped them out of the ice; we haven't yet inspected everything for fissionables or fusionables, or whatever makes those things explode. We haven't locked it all in a safe place where it won't get unstable, leak, or detonate.

# 12

• • •

# Return

It was windy when Pete left and started driving south. Wet brown and orange leaves churning up on the sides of the road seemed to fly at the new car, and the sky was a menacing slate gray. Pete drove down through Belfast and Augusta, then on through Portland and across New Hampshire and Massachusetts until, after Worcester, he dropped down into Connecticut and onto the Henry Hudson. Sometimes as he drove, Pete couldn't tell if the rain was outside or if it was his eyes. Grief flowed through him.

Alice had made him three tuna fish sandwiches on bagels for the drive and given him a thermos of coffee and two Ball jars full of water. He stopped in the woods and peed, as Alice had recommended he do, when he could, and otherwise just held it.

When he stopped for gas, he wore his mask and sanitized his hands once, twice, thrice. How many times would suffice? His eyes kept smarting.

Iris called on the phone, the name *Alice* popping up on the Bluetooth screen. "When are you coming back, Daddy?" she asked.

"As soon as I can, Pickle."

"Mommy's crying. And Sophie has gone off into the woods."

Pete felt like he was choking suddenly.

"Daddy, are you crying?" Pete could hear the shock in her voice, the desire to be corrected.

"No. I was just sneezing."

"Daddy?"

"Yes, Pickle."

"Are you going to get the Corona, Daddy?"

"No, Daddy will be very careful. Iris, the traffic is bad and it's raining. I need to hang up. But we will all be all right, Iris, don't worry. Daddy just has to go home to our apartment and do some work in the city. When I'm done, I'll see you again."

"Can you see if my cactus is still alive?"

"Of course, sweetie. I'll call you tomorrow, okay?"

"Okay. Bye, Daddy."

And then Pete was carried along by the traffic all around him and funneled as if on a water slide down the Hudson as Ryan Adams sang "New York, New York" on shuffle. He hadn't heard that song in so long; Alice wouldn't listen to Ryan Adams anymore. The highway finally spat him out at Seventy-Ninth Street. He turned left and pulled over on the corner and took a breath.

His hair was damp. His collar was damp. His underarms reeked. His chest felt sticky. He felt like he'd been out in the weather himself for the last eight and a half hours. When he let himself into the parking lot under their building, he felt the up and down in his stomach as he cleared the traffic bump, then smelled the familiar odors of concrete and gasoline coming through his window. It was a smell he loved. It smelled like home.

By the time he got inside the elevator, Pete felt repulsed by his own rank smell: his underarms and the stench of the tuna he had eaten as he drove was on his hands. He could smell onions and coffee on his breath inside his mask. He was carrying just a duffel bag with his running sneakers and a few random things he thought he'd need—some underwear and socks, as he was pretty sure Alice had taken all those to Maine; a T-shirt, two sweaters—and, in his other hand, his black leather bag that held his computer, iPad, phone, and some papers. Tucked in a pocket was the fern ID book Alice had given him for Father's Day. When he stepped out of the elevator and into the hall, he held his breath. It was empty, the blue carpet looking more worn than he remembered it. Holding his breath still, he opened their apartment door. It was dim inside. He let his bags drop on the sisal rug and pulled off his blue medical mask, breathing like a fish thrown clumsily back into the water after a long and cruel time on a dock. The familiarity of their lives soothed him. On both sides of the entry was the dark wooden shelving system that Alice had had custom made when they expanded into the next-door two-bedroom apartment, going from their 1,000-square-foot one-bedroom to the 2,400 square feet they now inhabited.

The thoughtful shelves and cabinets could hold everything from sneakers to bags, coats, and hats; anything one might need was neatly tucked away. Had he ever really looked carefully at this smart and thoughtful organization that framed their last few moments before they left in a hurry? Or, for that matter, their first few seconds after coming home? In Maine, the old house had quirks—it had only two original closets in the whole place, and all the work they had done on it had been created with the notion of two or three totally unencumbered, spare, and light-filled weeks in summer. There was no *real life* about their kitchen cabinets or the immense glass doors facing the ocean; everything was supposed to work against real life and was supposed to make you feel, instead, something like freedom.

Pete took his shoes off and padded into the dark apartment. The air smelled dry and stale. The gray light coming through the big plate-glass windows facing the Hudson showed him that a big pink geranium, several orchids, some waxy-looking things he couldn't identify, a fern, and several spidery-looking things were all dead, save a tiny bit of green on one orchid. A fig tree next to the wide, gray couch was also dead; the lime tree he had given Alice one year for Easter, also dead. He didn't feel anything about the plants, though he supposed he should. He went to the kitchen and got a cup of water for the one orchid that maybe had a chance, because he knew Alice would want him to. He poured it all in at once and went off to Iris's room to see if her cactus was still alive. It was, or it seemed to be. It was still green. On his way to get it some water, he heard a dripping sound coming from the living room and saw that all the water he had given the orchid had gone right through to the floor.

"Fuck." Grabbing a towel from the bathroom he got down on his knees and mopped up the water.

In the kitchen, he had seen mouse poop on the counters. The shiny wooden floors looked subdued; dust had settled everywhere. Pete could see his path back and forth to the plants and down the hall. Outside it was getting dark. Pete went around and turned on the lights in every room and then opened all the windows and got into the shower. "I can't do it all today," he told himself.

Clean, dressed, and warmer, Pete closed the windows and then ordered a pizza and found a bottle of wine in the wine vault off the pantry. It was red. He opened it and sat down on the couch as dust wafted from the cushions. He poured himself a glass and drank half of it in one gulp. His first instinct was to call the girls and Alice. But he hesitated. He was filled with doubt about where things stood: Would Alice answer? Where were they, in the existential sense? He poured some more wine and drank that. His stomach felt acidic and hungry and his hands were clammy. Down in his groin he knew he was headed in the wrong direction. It was like when the feeling to masturbate came over him. The impulse was distracting. The more he told himself it wasn't a good moment—he was cooking, shitting, exercising, talking to his daughters—the more impossible it was to avoid this ultimate conclusion; it was like a homing missile that could not be taken off course.

A third glass of wine and the doorbell rang. It was his pizza. A masked, gloved man stood at the door, wearing a navy-blue sweatshirt and a red cap with a pizza on it. Pete had forgotten his own mask. He extended his arm for the white box that already had a small seep of oil on the bottom left corner. "Thanks, man," Pete said, handing him an extra twenty. "Thanks," said the man, turning to go back down the hall toward the elevator, his shoulders, Pete noticed, making the perfect upside-down V, appearing to pull the man's body downward to the carpet.

"New York pizza," Pete murmured to himself. After he had eaten all but one of the slices, he stared at his phone. First the news about Amy Coney Barrett. She'd be confirmed no matter what. Alice must be losing her mind. Then the financial news. The markets were steady as they opened in Hong Kong. The girls would be going to bed soon. He knew he needed to call.

As he started to press on Alice's name, he stopped. He put his phone down and walked around the living room. Something about driving into the city, the excitement of being alone for the first time in eight months, was making a bubbly feeling in his chest. He wanted to contain it, but it thrummed, effervescent. He wanted to go out, drink beer, watch a movie, laugh with a friend. But what friend could go out with him and where? An age-old urge to party welled up in him, and even as he told himself it was silly, even immature, it was there, remarkably tingling all over his body, making him feel reckless. It was this part of him that Alice hated most; she liked calm and steady, normalcy. But Pete had this sparkle inside him, this bubbling champagne of heady desire that lodged itself just below his stomach. In Maine he had managed to tamp it down, contain it. What was it Alice called Sonja? The Her. So annoying.

On an impulse while looking out the window, he picked up his phone and texted: I am back. You in town? Free tonight? And then it was sent; the pin couldn't be pushed back into the grenade. He tried not to think of Alice or the girls. He felt nauseous and thrilled and scared. He couldn't watch the phone. Instead, he rushed down the hall to the bathroom to relieve himself, masturbating quickly and hard into the toilet. When he got back, there was a response.

In town. There was a photo in a large black-framed mirror: Sonja, naked, her long blond hair falling down her body, her hands on her nipples, and a black mask over her face.

My apartment?

Now?

God, yes.

Masked.

Like Eyes Wide Shut?

Exactly.

Kinky.

Pete texted his address.

\*   \*   \*

When they were done, they lay on their backs on Alice and Pete's bed. Pete said, "That was fucking awesome."

"My husband and I split up. I'm in New York full-time now."

Pete was silent. "Okay," he said. Like frost climbing up a

windowpane in winter, Pete felt a cold spread of anxiety fan into his limbs.

"We can get Covid tests, meet without the masks," she said.

Pete imagined meeting in his apartment; the apartment Alice had worked so hard to make a homey space. Did this woman have no morals? he felt himself, self-righteously, absurdly, wondering. He felt anger slide into his stomach like a slithery cobra. "I can't do this again," he said, the doors inside him shutting down and shame creeping from his toes up his body like a cold blanket. He closed his eyes. "I need to sleep. I'm exhausted."

Without speaking, Sonja slipped out of his bed, put her clothes on, and walked through the stale, dusty apartment. Pete imagined her seeing the kids' bedrooms, the dead plants, the pictures on the walls, the dark wooden shelves by the door. Quietly, Pete heard Sonja open the door and she went out and, presumably, down the hall and back into the city.

When Pete awoke, his mask stuck to his sticky breath, he immediately smelled Sonja's perfume. It seemed to linger uncomfortably under his mask. It was earthy and exotic smelling, a thin hint underneath of burning plastic. His cheeks burned as he thought back to the hours before. His falling asleep bothered him the most; his lack of remorse, his body's willingness to soothe itself, even now. He felt his stomach roil. He ran to the bathroom and threw up. In the gray light of early morning, Pete heaved until nothing was left. His head hung over the toilet until he felt himself start to cry. He tried to remember the last time he had cried—like really *cried*—when his mother died? He didn't think so. He must have been a boy. The feeling was almost startling, as tears flowed out of his eyes and stung his face, slipping into his open vomit-tasting mouth, from which an unearthly and uncontrollable sound emanated. But there was something wonderful about it too. He let himself sob over the toilet until no more sound and no more liquids came from him.

Pete got into the shower and cleaned his body. Then he came out, walked past his children's rooms, and averted his gaze. He couldn't look. He went to his closet and carefully got dressed in a suit and shirt and tie. He laced up his shoes. He pulled a wad of medical masks out of a box Alice had preemptively gotten from a friend who was a surgeon and left in the kitchen all those months ago, not thinking they would need them in Maine. He put all but one in his pocket; the last he put on his face. He got into the elevator and went down to the lobby.

The day doorman, Tito, wearing a thick black mask, saw him.

"Long time no see, Mr. Pete!" Tito exclaimed.

"Hi, Tito. We've been in Maine."

"Where's the missus? Those little girls?" Tito's gray hair looked silver in the light. Pete wondered if Tito had been working last night too. He couldn't remember Tito's schedule all of a sudden. Was Tito playing him right now? Did he see Sonja? Who let her in? It was the new guy, Alexei, he thought. But what if Tito was just coming on for the overnight?

Pete couldn't breathe inside the mask. He cleared his throat and walked through the door Tito was holding open to the outside, until in the fresh air he could pull the mask down to get a breath.

"They're still in Maine, Tito. I'm back for some work."

"Okay, Pete the Cat. Have a good day."

"What did you call me?" Pete felt huffy.

"Like the cat, man. The kids' book? Don't worry—you good." And Tito was laughing a big broad good-natured laugh.

\* \* \*

Pete bought a coffee on the street, and since it was early he decided to walk as long as his feet could handle it; how else was anyone getting anywhere these days? he wondered. He pulled his mask around his chin so he could breathe. It felt good to be back in the city, as empty as it was. Everything, even the air, felt normal.

# 13

• • •

# Thanksgiving

Late at night, Sophie can hear Alice leaving messages. It is a week and then two and then her mother takes them to vote in an old grange hall and then it's Thanksgiving. Her father is still gone. Sophie watches the calendar with a renewed interest, checking off the days in her head. Days seem to slide by, never getting them anywhere new.

Sophie hears Alice leaving those messages when she thinks Sophie and Iris are dead to the world. Her voice, over those first few days, graduates from sounding casual to insistent to alarmed to irate. Then she stops calling, as far as Sophie can tell. Eventually, Pete calls and speaks to Sophie and Iris and he and Alice have curt exchanges. What happened in between the messages and those new phone calls, Sophie has no idea. But the feeling of it lodges somewhere between her sternum and her stomach, a hard ball of something icky, like a rotten turnip. At night, Sophie thinks that if she can stay awake long enough and witness and listen, puzzle it together, somehow she might be able to control what happens. Help. Say the right thing. Something. It's been months of watching her parents unknit; now it seems those last dangling strands are being cut. There is a helplessness Sophie feels that makes her want to throw up, chew her fingers to the quick until they bleed, cut all her hair off, pick every tiny blackhead she can find on her nose, pinch her thigh until it bruises.

The day before Thanksgiving, Alice tells Sophie and Iris that she needs to go shopping for Thanksgiving dinner. She asks Sophie to stay with Iris, watching *Geronimo Stilton*. That is the only way Sophie can babysit, with a screen to anesthetize Iris. Otherwise Iris is a total nightmare and Sophie manages to swing back to her own inner six-year-old. Sophie watches Alice walk out the door and then turns back to the screen and the smugly velvet voice of Geronimo, the mouse reporter. "Iris, you realize that as soon as she's gone, I'm not sitting here and watching this."

"I'll tell Mommy."

"I'll tell her about the marshmallows you ate."

Then Sophie turns away and watches her mother duck into the car. It is raining. Through the wide picture window on her left that looks out to the driveway she can see the old lilacs, now standing gray and scabby against the wet sky. She sees Alice put her hands on the steering wheel and then take them off quickly, as if it's hot or made of ice, and then sees her pull on the red knitted mittens she bought at a craft sale. Sophie watches her mother turn on the car and the headlights and then fiddle with what Sophie imagines is the radio, NPR most likely, and then she sees her mother drive away. Next to her, Iris is eating a bagel with cream cheese and tomatoes on it.

In October, her mother pulled the last of the green tomatoes from the vines and spread them out on cookie sheets. She put them upstairs in the hall on the little table where she normally puts flowers. In the warm afternoon light, they've been turning red, and every night, they have a fresh tomato with dinner as if it were August. Sophie wondered, but never asked, how her mother knew to do that. Since coming to Maine her mother seemed to figure out all kinds of things that Sophie didn't know she was able to do: like gardening and cooking large elaborate meals using the *New York Times* cooking app. In New York, her mother had always "deferred to the experts," she liked to say, in matters of cuisine. Now, she was teaching herself to be an expert, ever since those strange weeks of almost going insane eating cereal and olives. These days, everything Alice made seemed to involve some ginger and garlic frying, which made the house smell amazing, but always took forever. When Sophie told Alice she was starving, Alice would say absent-mindedly, "Hmm-hmm. It'll be ready soon—says here forty-five minutes, but that's bullshit. Any recipe from the *Times* that involves ginger and garlic frying, add another hour. Have some crackers, Sophs."

Even though Sophie knows that she won't do as her mother has asked and stay with Iris on the couch, she lingers an extra moment, feeling worried her mother might reappear like some

Harpy. Then Sophie mutters, "Fuck that," under her breath and smirks at her grown-up language. "Iris," she interrupts. "Iris! PICKLE! Darn it. I'm hitting pause. Iris, I'm going upstairs. You good?"

"Uh-huh," says Iris, all sweet and docile now from the screen. Almost lovable if you don't remember what a terror she is.

Sophie goes upstairs, tiptoeing on the steps, though there is no need to be so secretive; Iris is laughing at Geronimo and Thea and Trap, and nothing else matters. Trap is Iris's favorite, the lovable, fat loser-mouse who gets everything wrong and irritates the shit out of Geronimo.

When Sophie reaches the top of the stairs, she stops: wide boards on the floor, the blue throw rugs have been crumpled and shoved to the side, revealing worn patches from their family always, *always* being home. Dust and hair and dirt bloom out by two inches or more from the sides of the hall. But other than that, sunlight is now coming through the south-facing window at the end of the hall, slicing through the November sky that seemed, just an hour ago, determined to stay gray and dank. The unexpected shard of light illuminates the tomatoes like they are being painted just in front of her by one of those old Italian painters her mother loves so much at the Met that she could stand there, annoyingly, forever, commenting on the light and dark space. The light makes this white-walled passage with the dark mahogany banister spindles seem almost glorious. Sophie feels a fleeting moment of joy, like a small bird inside her chest has revived after being kept captive inside a dark box. In her head she hears Paul McCartney's voice, "I've got a feeling, a feeling deep inside, oh yeah, oh yeah . . ." and she feels a warmth spread through her body and down to the secret place between her legs. It makes her feel woozy for a second. "I've got a feeling, a feeling I can't hide, oh no, oh no, oh no . . ."

Sophie found a Discman in the closet in the front foyer a few weeks ago and a stack of old CDs. One of them was *Let It Be*. For weeks now, she has listened over and over to the album, "I've Got a Feeling" stuck forever in her head, the line about the wet dream shocking and thrilling her. Then she found the photos on the internet of Paul and John in their last performance on that roof, more photos of Paul in the studio looking impossibly handsome.

Alone in the hallway, she considers going to her room to be alone and to listen to "I've Got a Feeling" with the door shut. But time—she isn't sure she has enough of it. How long will their mother be gone? It's unclear to her how long these things take—forever, five minutes? It's not yet cemented in her brain the way it will be one day, when she has grown and done the same errand thousands of times, until it's just second nature to estimate the timing of things.

Waiting for a second longer in the hall, Sophie decides to move along with her mission, the flushed feeling between her thighs dissipating to the sound of her heart beating. She can't waste time today thinking about Paul McCartney. She pushes the door to her mother's bedroom open, the room they all end up in every night.

The windows are shut, and the covers thrown back where they left them, a blanket peeking out of the closet where Sophie makes a mat in the middle of the night. The air still smells like morning breath and dreams. Three glasses of water, all partially drunk, at different levels, sit on the bedside table next to the lamp. Each glass has what looks like white powder stuck to the insides. Minerals in the water, her mother tells her. Left behind when the water evaporates. "What is *evaporates*?" asks Iris. Iris asks the stupidest questions. She wants concrete definitions to things that just *are*. "Great question," says Alice, irritating Sophie even more. "*Evaporates* means it goes into the air in tiny droplets that we can't see, disappearing." Sophie feels grumpy just thinking about it now.

In a little nook, looking out a low window to the west and the gardens, is her mother's desk. It is dark wood and ornately carved and has drawers all over it. Her mother keeps the iPad in there. Once a day, Sophie is allowed to get on it for an hour to Snapchat with Isla and Robin and Eloise. They tell her about meeting in the park with masks and how their parents let them take their masks down if they sit on different nearby benches and talk from there. How sometimes they forget and go sit next to one another until one of their mothers notices and tells them they have to spread out again. They tell Sophie about how school is still online and how much they hate math and how Mrs. Parker is always muting herself on Zoom so they have no idea what she's telling them about the book they're reading, *The Giver*. They tell her about Nick Feinberg and Justin Azurro and how Justin's voice makes these ridiculous crackly sounds and sometimes sounds deep and other times high. They tell her that lately they can go out and get ice cream on the street and stand six feet apart and eat it together. Sophie listens to all of it. But when they ask her, "How's Maine?" Sophie has no idea how to explain. She can't think of the words to show them what it's like being outside all day; how the ocean crashes on the shore and how it's so loud she can't even hear her own thoughts when she's down at the end of the yard; she can't explain the trees and what they feel like to climb in her cold, bare feet, or what it's like to see the field turn orange and brown after it was so green. She can't explain how wide the blue sky is and how free it makes her feel to look up at it, but also so small. She can't explain the ferns, or the sumac's red berries.

A couple of times recently, early in the morning, Sophie has awoken in the closet to find her mother siting there at her desk, looking out the window. She has a legal pad in front of her and a pen. Her face is wet with tears. When she sees Sophie, she shoves the notebook into the low, wide middle drawer and smiles. "Hello, Button." It is that legal pad Sophie is after now. She opens the drawer and sees it, the pen sitting on top. On the other side of the drawer is the iPad, its screen darkened. For a moment Sophie considers taking the iPad out and seeing if Eloise or Robin can Snapchat. She might get more than an hour with her mother gone. No one will ever know. She picks it up and presses down on the button on the side. The apple illuminates. As she waits she looks down at the legal pad and sees her mother's loopy handwriting across the page and remembers. She shoves the iPad back in the drawer, forgetting that she has left it on and her mother will know. She picks up the legal pad and takes it inside the closet, closes the door, clicks on her little purple plastic reading lamp that she keeps next to her cot, and plops down on her covers. She reads in her mother's crabby handwriting:

*A LIST*:

*REASONS I SHOULD LEAVE PETE, PROS & CONS.*

| CONS: | PROS: |
|---|---|
| the girls. | he will never change. |
| the house(s) | he loves my girls. |
| i still love him. | he says he loves me. |
| i want to forgive him. | i do think he loves me. |
| when we are good, our family is good. | he is human. |
| he has always made me uneasy with other women. he makes me uneasy, period. | he is evolving. |
| he lies. he has always lied. mostly little things. i think. now a big thing. | i don't really know what happened when we got married or why we got married, it's all sort of blurry for me. |
| something is missing. i don't know what the something is. does everyone feel this? | he betrayed me. |
| people can change. i think. | it could be more than once. i don't know. |
| | he betrayed my girls. (right?) |

i don't know if forgiveness is
real.
i will never trust him.
i will never trust him.
i will never trust him.
i will never trust him.

Sophie takes this list in. She breathes heavily. She remembers, suddenly, a time at the end of a summer when she and her parents went out to Nantucket Island. She must have been five or so. Her mother was huge and pregnant with Iris. A friend of her father's was getting married and they went out for the wedding. They were staying in a sprawling gray-shingled house right on the dunes, Sophie remembers, and she had to wear a white dress with a blue satin ribbon around the waist, and she couldn't get the dress dirty in the sand before the ceremony, which was going to be on the beach. It was hot and sunny and she remembers just wanting to sit down in the water, the dress be damned, and let the waves crash onto her legs and make them feel cool. After the ceremony, they had to traipse back up that hot, dry beach, and they sat at round plastic tables with yellow tablecloths and ate filet mignon and long skinny green beans that had a funny name and then there was a huge coconut cake and her father drank champagne.

That night, she and her mother went to bed after the cake and her father stayed at the party, which was in a great big room, and there were flowers everywhere in vases and there were these wide sliding doors out to a porch, and, just beyond that, was that magnificent blond-colored beach, and after that, her dad said, was ocean and more ocean and then England. Sophie remembers that that big room had pretty china all around it, on shelves and the mantelpiece and on side tables, all gleaming and white, and when she picked up one of the little painted bowls, she saw on the bottom of it that same word, *England*, and she remembers thinking about how that china had come all the way over that ocean and up over the dunes to that house.

Anyway, Sophie remembers her mother falling asleep quickly and she was not able to sleep because of the laughter and music downstairs. So after a little while Sophie got up and went to the stairs and started to make her way down to find her father. But just as she got to the bottom of the stairs and was about to cross a little room with a small bar and two light-green-colored couches and a lamp her mother had told her was made out of whalebone, she remembers seeing her father with a drink in a plastic cup in one hand and his other arm around a woman with long red hair, and they were dancing, but very close, and her father's hand was on that woman's bare back. That's all she remembers. Standing on the stairs and looking across the little room into the big room. Sophie sat down. And then felt weird inside and went back upstairs to the room, where her mother had fallen asleep. She crawled in next to her mother's huge, hot body. There wasn't much more to this memory except that Sophie felt breathless for a little while, and guilty, like she was a bad girl and had done something she shouldn't. Finally she started to breathe along with her mother's breaths and then she fell asleep.

Holding her mother's notebook, Sophie feels that breathless feeling again. She looks around the room. She is uncomfortable, suddenly, with learning the details in her mother's mind. She wants to put it back, get it out of her hands. Downstairs she hears Iris's little feet get up and run to the kitchen. She knows that Iris is now climbing on the counters and is getting into the large glass jar they put sweet stuff in to keep the ants out, and she is looking for the marshmallows. Iris thinks no one will know. But they always know because she leaves the cap off, or the marshmallow bag empty and on the counter. She is not yet practiced enough in the art of deception. She leaves trails of breadcrumbs.

Panicked suddenly, Sophie rips the list off of the pad and balls it up, and then stiffens, unsure now of what to do. "I shouldn't have done that," she mutters. "Ergh." Nancy Drew and her smart, methodical decisions looms up in Sophie's mind.

She impulsively takes the balled-up paper and starts to eat it, ripping pieces of the paper off and chewing them and swallowing. After three swallows, she goes to the nightstand and rinses her throat with the stale water. What a dumb thing I'm doing, she thinks. There is so much more paper in her hand. She keeps going. Now that she's started she has to finish. After ten swallows, the ball is much smaller, small enough, she figures, to go down the toilet, and so she rushes out into the hall and into the bathroom and flushes it down. Relief spreads over her that she no longer needs to eat any more paper and that all the evidence is gone.

But then she remembers the empty legal pad she left on her

mother's bed when she was eating the paper and drinking the last dregs of water in the glasses. She rushes back to the room and picks it up. She doesn't know what to do with it now, but she knows she needs to get it out of her mother's room. Keeping it in her hand and taking one more look through the door and at this room full of the suspended sweetness of bedtime, the light falling on the clean cotton sheets, the white comforter, the puritanical white painted boards on the floor, she rushes out into the hall and throws the legal pad through Iris's doorway so that her mother will think Iris took it. Then she heads downstairs, calling, "Iris, I know what you are doing! Iris, you bad girl poop."

Iris, back on the couch, turns, her mouth full of sticky white marshmallow, a bit of which is squeezing out the corner of her small mouth. "Ha-ha, I caught you," Sophie says.

"Don't tell Mama," Iris says reflexively, chewing thoughtfully and locking in on Sophie with that gaze that is so unnaturally confident it disarms Sophie at times.

The girls are staring at each other again. Time stops, the way it can with kids. There is no clock ticking anywhere. It's a silence that comes between children who get lost in their own dreams and thoughts and faraway places. This realm is never understood by adults. When silence descends, her mother will ask, what are you two *doing*? As if it portends an impending storm, or something naughty. Sometimes, she is right. Silence can mean that Iris has stolen off to do something she shouldn't. Or silence can mean that Sophie has vanished from the task she was given and gone to her room to lose herself in *My Friend*

*Flicka*, and she's deep in imagining that she is far, far away, riding a horse across the wilds of Wyoming. But more often than not, it means that the girls are breathing together, island-hopping from dream to dream like little Amelia Earharts, soaring above blue water.

Now, after a discernible breath and a last swallow of marsh-mallow, Iris says, "Did you know that Daddy put his penis inside Mommy's half butt to make a baby and Mommy said it felt good?"

"Iris, you're a moron. It's not her half butt. You're not three anymore. It's her vagina. Like you have. The hole in the middle."

"What does the vagina do again?"

"Hold penises and make babies."

"Hold penises? Like a vase holds flowers? Like . . . a hand holds a carrot?"

"Yeah, something like that, Poop."

"And then there's the vulva," Iris continues.

"Iris. My God. No one needs the anatomy lesson."

Silence. Iris fidgets with the remote, then picks her nose. "I'm thirsty."

"Drink."

Iris hops down off the couch and gets herself a glass and fills it with water. Then, "You're a terrible babysitter."

"Okay, Poop," Sophie says, still standing, now looking out the window, hoping her mother will come home, bustle in with packages and false cheer to fill up the lonely space of silence that seems to permeate every inch of their lives in Maine. All the constant noise and chaos of New York is gone in this one long, interminable pause. "This is a short blip in our lives," her mother tells her. "If you read, you will be fine," she says, and hands Sophie another book. After the Nancy Drew series, Sophie read the entire dog-eared and cat-puke-tan-covered Trixie Belden series, left by the old lady who owned the house before them; she's reread Harry Potter, moved on to *Where the Red Fern Grows*, then *Old Yeller* and *Black Beauty* and then *Treasure Island*, *Watership Down*, and *The Yearling*, which she got halfway through, then realized it might never end.

Anything, though, with adventure or animals, or both. Now she scans the adult books. Her eyes light upon *Ulysses* by James Joyce. One time in summer in New York, her mother took her to Symphony Space and they heard a woman with a long Irish name that Sophie remembers as sounding like *Fin-ooh-laaaa* (was that possible?) read out loud from a big thick book also called *Ulysses*, which was based on the story of Odysseus, her mother told her. Alice told Sophie that the Fin-ooh-laaaa woman was going to read that book out loud all day long and all night long too. Sophie tried to imagine what it would be like if her own parents read to her for that long. Would she stay awake? She remembers her mother saying, "Gosh, her mouth must get so dry." Alice and Sophie didn't stay that long. Alice said, "Who could stay for the entire thing? Not one audience member." But the snippet they did hear, Sophie now remembers, had a line about breasts being "all sweet perfume." Sophie remembers that line and looks down at her own breasts, which have started to flop a bit when she runs in a most disconcerting manner. "Flopping should be banned," she says out loud but not meaning to.

Iris looks at her, bemused. It's reassuring to Iris when her sister says weird thoughts out loud; she's not the only one who is odd, and that's comforting. Then she asks, "Is Daddy ever coming back?"

"Of course," says Sophie. "I mean. I don't know, Poop."

"Stop calling me that."

"Stop being a poop."

"Will Daddy get Covid in New York at his job?"

"Oh, probably."

"Probably?"

"Yes, Poop, that's what I said."

"Oh, poor Daddy."

"Mama's back."

Both girls turn to see Alice pull up to the house. The light outside is fading and they both need to squint to see their mother through the windshield. Her headlights are on and they stream into the house, mixing with the dying light from across the water and making the room look sepulchral.

Iris says, "I'm going to help Mama."

"You just want to see what's in the bags."

"Yes," says Iris and pulls on her coat.

For a moment, Sophie stands alone in the house. Outside she can hear Iris squeaking to her mother and car doors being shut. She feels an odd combination of guilt for not helping and relief not to be helping, thankful that Iris is taking this burden on today. After a moment, Sophie grabs her coat. It's taking too long. What are they doing out there? She pulls on her boots and without zipping anything opens the door. Her mother and Iris are standing in front of the car that's now quietly ticking as it cools down. Iris holds a small paper bag and Alice holds two bulging with food. But they are looking at the last shreds of light across water. Stripes of deep rosy-fingered dusk and hot orange follow the bulge of the sun as it slides under the water. As Sophie is standing there and watching her mother and Iris watch the sun, it is gone, and the light has died along with it. Alice turns then and sees her older daughter in the doorway, hair in a snarly ponytail, stained leggings, jacket open to reveal a worn old Beatles T-shirt, face sallow. And Sophie sees her mother smile, the last golden shard hitting her hair, her mother's face full of wonder and love and happiness to see her. And in that moment, Alice, in turn, witnesses the power of her own smile, the unsure look of her daughter soften to relief, a face that brings Alice back to Sophie at three and four, when she was their only child and everything was new and uncharted territory, and this daughter's presence was the thin squeeze of glue that kept them together, kept her sane.

"Sophie," she calls across the dusky light of the driveway that separates them. "I got so much food. We're going to have the best meal tomorrow!"

"Oh good," Sophie says. And then a look of sorrow passes over Sophie's face even before she feels it inside, even before she can articulate to herself what she already knows, which is that her mother is smiling to make it better in a situation that is not better and can't be made better, or at least not right now, and not in time for the holiday tomorrow. Alice sees her daughter's light extinguish as fast as it shone, and she wants to put her bags down and run after Sophie and shake her, tell her to hold on to the light, that it will all be okay. Sophie can see that Alice feels shame and anger, that she knows that she herself is a part of the darkness that crushes her daughters. And for a second Sophie wants to open up, talk, let tears fall down her cheeks. But then, Sophie sees something else flash across Alice's face: *defiance* would be the word, if Sophie could retrieve it.

Sophie turns and slides back inside, takes off her boots, hangs her coat back up, and slips into the downstairs bathroom and shuts the door. She feels a jagged breath in her chest and shuts her eyes against the force of a wave, building momentum and threatening to thrash the few delicate sticks that make a raft that holds her afloat day in and day out. She presses her fingers tight against her eyes until they ache, and she thinks she might damage the soft jelly underneath.

"Sophs," Alice calls, stomping inside.

"Be right there," Sophie says and means it. She splashes cool water on her face, dries it, and tries to find a place inside her to shove the buckets of watery grief that seem to brim and overflow at the world's worst moments. A hunk of something that stings like bile lodges in her throat and can't be swallowed. Leaving it there, she goes out into the kitchen.

"Let's start a pie," Alice says and hands Sophie flour and butter and a bag of apples. And they begin: slicing, rolling, pressing, and measuring until the whole house smells like apples and cinnamon and allspice and everything is almost right.

# 14

• • •

# Winter

It's gotten cold. Not impossible cold, but cold. The sky is low and dark overhead and the waves are gray and the foam is white, spraying high up into the sky against the granite rocks, like I'm in a Winslow Homer painting. On the edges of the shore, seafoam has frozen on top of the sand; it looks like a wrinkled sheet, left in a hurry on an unmade bed. In winter, this world has become ours.

Pete has been gone now for six weeks. Our phone calls are short; he mostly talks to the girls. It's like this thing just happened. I don't even know what it was, really. He left and we entered a nowhere zone. I don't know if we are separated or not. Time is stopped. Even as the virus rages on, even as the election is decided, and decided, and decided again (thank God). I am suspended day after day, week after week, month after month, living and not living my life at the same time. Thanksgiving came and went as a nothing holiday with a roast chicken and some cranberry sauce. I was able to explain Pete's absence to the girls in terms of Covid. I think they bought it.

It is hard for me to warm the house up. The fireplace wood is long gone. I have put space heaters in all the rooms; they make the air sizzle and give off an acrid burned-rubber smell. The girls are inside more, fighting, lying around, making little cairns of their things all over the house. Without discussing it, we all have migrated into my bed to sleep. I say good night to Iris, and then Sophie and I plop down together on the couch to watch *The Great British Bake Off*. After Sophie is in bed, I go out to the couch by myself to read or watch something mindless, once again. I gave up on *Borgen* after the husband, Philip, cheated on the prime minister, his wife. I watched a show about arranged marriages in India for a time. Then, even that became too much for my addled brain at night.

I wait until the darkness feels like it is pressing on all sides of the house, and the lonely sounds of wind and waves become too much for me to bear, and then I fold myself into the bed with my children, feeling childlike myself, and scared. Iris sleeps in the middle, Sophie on the far side next to the window. Each night, sometime in the darkness, Sophie migrates to the mat she has set up in my closet; somehow she curls her body into the tight space and pulls a sleeping bag over herself, like a chipmunk hibernating. In the morning, I find myself clutching Iris's small body for comfort, pulling her knees into the spoon I make with my body, my arms tight around her back, my breath dampening her hair.

We wake together, our blankets tangled and hot, Sophie unfurling into the room with an angry expression on her face, and I stumble into the kitchen to make coffee and breakfast. It's odd how without Pete here, without school, without even the pretense of school, and as Covid has removed any real errands or anywhere to be on time or late for, or to be sick for, for that matter, there is no real reason to our days, no schedule. Without Pete needing to work, at the very least, we are even more in a dream state, the girls and I. We read, we eat, we go outside for hours and hours investigating every nook and cranny of this land we never knew before. Sometimes, I work with Iris on the alphabet and throw Sophie a real-life math problem to solve. Lately, we talk about Christmas. The girls are making and remaking their Santa lists.

"Will Daddy be here for Christmas?" Iris asks me. At first I don't respond. I busy myself with the sandwiches I am making for lunch; I cut them in perfect triangles and cut up carrots to go alongside. She asks again.

"I think so, honey," I say and try to give a reassuring smile.

Sophie is lying on a couch, her feet up, looking at a magazine. She folds the magazine toward her chest and gives me a dark look. "Why do you say it like that? My God! I *hate* you. Daddy's only gone to New York. You act like he's never coming back to us."

"I'm sorry," I say. Though I need to say more. What would the right combination of things be to say to my children? What words must I summon to explain this limbo and not scare them or fill them with false hope?

Snow comes plentifully just before Christmas, shawling out of the sky, blanketing everything but the black water, making it look like the end of our yard drops off into oblivion. The girls squeal and go outside as I make pancakes. Pancakes, pancakes, that is all we eat. Every morning. The only food Iris will allow; the warm sweet of them goes down her gullet easily, without a fight, which is a mercy.

The pancakes are ready just as I look out and see Sophie give Iris a white wash and Iris emerge, covered in white snow, furious and punching.

When they are inside and out of their wet gear, they ask to talk to Daddy. I set them up to FaceTime with Pete. I hear them tell Pete all about the snow, how white it is, how clean, how perfect, how different from New York City snow, which gets dirty much too fast and never comes so plentifully. My heart longs to share with him too—the glittering snow, the pancakes, the white wash, the fighting, and how incredibly fucking fatiguing it all is. But just as Sophie hands me the phone, I feel cloudy, angry.

"Hi, Pete," I say with an edge. I feel a searing, charring anger when I hear his voice, and yet, inscrutably, I want him here. I don't understand these two feelings; they make no sense, colliding in the same moments and making me feel bipolar.

As soon as he drove away, it was all fresh and hot for me. I wanted those early days in Maine back, when we hung together so closely, even though I'm not sure now they were real. The children, I think, the children. Snap out of it for the children. Yet somehow even the tug of their faces, their actual bodies next to mine, their voices and tears, can't pull me back from the reckless anger I feel whenever I hear his voice.

"Hi, Alice."

"How's work?"

"Strange. Normal. The same. Masked. Alice—"

"Not now."

"We need to talk about Christmas, Alice. And it looks like we are going fully remote again."

"I can call you tonight."

"You say that and then you never call. You don't respond to texts."

"I will call."

I hear a sigh. It irritates me. I hang up before there's any more. Sophie is glaring at me.

"Shall we go try skiing later today, girls?" I smile.

"Fine," says Sophie.

"Yippee!" says Iris. "We're going to spend the whooooole day outside in the snow, Mommy."

I've found some old skis and snowshoes in the barn and a cardboard box with ski boots. Both Sophie and I fit into the skis. After lunch, I pack up tin mugs and a thermos of hot chocolate into my backpack, and I will pull Iris behind in a sled I ordered from L.L.Bean.

When we get outside, Sophie and I look around and she asks, "Which way?"

"Over the field, how about? *And through the woods.*" I sing those last few words. Sophie glares at me. "Okay." I sober up; no singing. But then: "How about *and along by our favorite tree*?" (I can't help myself. I like annoying her.) "We can stop there and have the hot chocolate."

Sophie heads off in that general direction.

Immediately it's a disaster. The skis need goop on them or we need special snow, or these are just too old. They keep getting gunked up with snow that makes them stick and then slip. We are falling on our asses, Sophie and I, Iris sliding away from me in the sled down the rises in the field, pulling me backward. It's like something from a Chris Van Dusen book. By the time we get to the woods, we are panting and soaking and Sophie is hurling insults back at me as I follow in her messy wake.

"I *hate* you," she yells. "You're a bad mom and a terrible person." Iris is crying in the sled and all I want is for both of them to just vanish for ten minutes so that I can catch my breath in this cold heaven by myself and come back better. Sophie yanks off her skis at the woods' edge and picks up the poles and skis and starts chucking them willy-nilly into the snow and yells, "I hate you and I never want to see you again," and takes off into the woods. Iris is screaming, "Wait! Sophie, wait!" Iris gets out of the sled and takes off after her sister in her thick, bulky snowsuit. "Good, get lost, both of you," I mutter, honestly not caring whether or not they can hear me, and pulling off my own skis, I leave them in a pile with the poles next to a yellow birch.

When I get into the woods, I can hear Iris screeching for Sophie to wait and I can follow their footsteps. I arrive at our big old white pine and find them both waiting. The front of Iris's coat is soaked from crying and snot seeps out of her nose. I have no tissues; another strike against me. I use my mitten and clean her face. Sophie has climbed up into the tree and is chucking snow at both Iris and me. We are dodging it. Iris is hysterical and in retaliation is hurling large handfuls of snow up into the tree without packing it into any balls, and it is only coming back down onto both of us.

"Jesus Christ, Sophie," I yell. "Goddammit! Cut it out. Enough. Iris, stop warbling. I can't think."

Sophie yells, "I hate you and I hate her and I wish you both would just evaporate."

I take a breath. A mother must stand still for her children, or something like that. *Bridges of Madison County*. Meryl Streep made it look easy. Then again, it was written by a man—a man's idea of what a mother should do. Even so, "Stand still," I tell myself. But all I want to do is take off running and raving like a lunatic. I feel myself almost foaming at the mouth.

"I understand," I say, trying to tamp down anything else that could come out and I'd regret. I want to put my head down in the snow and look up into these big pine boughs and cry until night comes.

It is silent except for Iris sniffling. I can't stand the sound, but I try to steady myself with my eyes on the tree.

"I want Daddy," Sophie says. Now the tsunami begins. She is sobbing. "I have heard you at night. I heard you fighting before we left the city. I heard you calling and leaving messages. I've heard him calling at night and you not answering. I know he loves someone else. I know what happened. And I know you're never letting him come back here and we're never going to see him again and we have nothing here. No friends, no Dad. No school. All we do is the same thing over and over and over; nothing changes. We're in this house day after day after day. Day after day we eat pancakes because that's what Iris wants."

"Mommy, Daddy loves someone else? Does he have other daughters?"

"No, Iris, no. It's not like that. Goddammit, Sophie. Thank you very much."

"See, I knew you'd yell at me! I *hate* you. Daddy is right to love someone else. You are a horrible, ugly, mean, terrible person."

"Sophie, you little bitch!" It comes out of my mouth before I even know what I am saying. I *hate* myself.

For what seems like an eternity I am silent and I can hear that infernal sniffling of Iris's. If I tune that out as best I can, I hear the snow falling onto the boughs of the tree. How can I explain this? How can I retrieve my daughter in the tree who knows too much and also protect the snot-covered one next to me? The last thing I want to do is protect Pete. But I realize I have to. And I hate him for it.

"Girls," I begin, haltingly. "Love is . . . complicated. Big people don't always do the best job at it. Relationships take work. Sometimes big people get tired of doing the work or can't figure out how to do the work and then sometimes they make mistakes because someone else seems easier. Daddy loves you both very much. He doesn't have any other daughters. Only you two and he's devoted to you. Right now Daddy and I have to figure out if we can love each other the way we used to. I know it's a lot for both of you and it's hard and unfair that you have to be on this train with us."

"You're right, it's not fair," yells Sophie.

"Sophie, listen. I am sorry. It's a hard time right now. It will get better. The world is upside down. *We* are upside down. But we will be okay. I will do better. We can do better."

"Mommy?"

"Not now, Iris. Sophie, did you hear me?"

"Mommy?"

"Iris! What?"

"I peed my pants, Mommy."

"You dummy, Iris." The tree speaks.

"Stop it, Sophie. It's the stress. Let's go home, guys. We can have the hot chocolate in the house. We can talk more about this there."

Silence.

"No. I'm not coming down. You promised hot chocolate at the tree."

"You promised, Mommy," says Iris.

"Iris, you're all wet. Aren't you too cold to have the hot chocolate here?"

"No."

"See, you idiot," Sophie lobs down at me.

I dole out the hot chocolate, handing Sophie's tin mug up to her as Iris sits on the snow, making a little yellow imprint where her pee-soaked pants touch the white. We drink in silence. I collect the mugs. Sophie comes down, tearstained and with a mustache of chocolate around her mouth. We trudge out of the woods and home, me carrying the wet Iris. We leave the skis and sled in the snow.

The lights are on when we come across the dark field. The windows look like yellow eyes.

"The house looks like a friend," says Iris.

"It *is* our friend," I say.

Ingmar is waiting for us by the door when we come in. He purrs and rubs against our legs, reminding us that it's dinnertime. "Yes, yes," I tell him. "Give me a few minutes to get the girls set up."

I take Iris into the bathroom and run her a "shower bath." "Mommy," she says, as I pull off her underwear. "I'm sorry. But . . . I pooped a little bit in my pants too."

"It's okay, Pickle. That was a hard time. Let's wipe you up and get you in the warm water." When I come out, Sophie is on the couch.

I sit down next to her and put my hand on her knee. "I love you."

"I hate you."

"I am sorry. I can imagine that for you at this age knowing what you know is very hard. I still love Daddy. But I am very angry and hurt."

"You didn't act angry and hurt all summer when he was here."

"I know. I mean, I was. Honestly. But less. I don't know what happened. I got angry as soon as he left. Or I got scared. That can make a person angry."

"I want Daddy back."

She is my little girl again, and her shoulders are heaving as

I pull her to me. Her tears fall hot on my neck and down my sweater. "I know, Pumpkin. I know. I do too."

After a bit, she says, "And I hate Iris. She bothers me all the time and steals my books and rips my drawings and kicks me when I'm sleeping so I need to sleep in the closet and I *hate* her."

"I understand. Being a big sister is a hard job. You are a wonderful big sister."

"And I'm hungry."

"Let's make a frozen pizza. Want to help?" She nods. Her softness now is like a needle in my heart, as the poem goes.

She unwraps the plastic and finds the pan. Her courage and ability to go forward right now, when all I want to do is go stick my head under the covers, makes me want to weep.

"Salad?" I ask.

She nods. I pull out the greens and wash them. "You make the dressing." I watch her pour olive oil and balsamic into the bowl like I taught her. Then a pinch of salt and pepper. I realize I've lost track of what a lady she is becoming, how long and delicate her neck is, how capable her hands.

Later, after we have eaten, and the house is warm and we are full, we all get into the bed together. Both girls are breathing heavily within minutes. In the dark, I know I need to go back out to the kitchen. I need to clean up so tomorrow morning is easier. I need to call Pete like I promised. I need to shower myself. But oh, if I could only stay here a little longer, a little longer in this soft, warm envelope of sweetness next to my innocent children.

When I come to, it's after eleven. The lights are still on in the living room and kitchen. I don't feel like calling Pete. I want a bath. I survey the messy kitchen. I just can't attempt it right now. "After," I tell myself, "I'll call him."

When the bath is run, I drop a little lavender in the water. I get in and lie back. The water feels like a cocoon; I get back that warm, safe feeling I had in the dark with the kids breathing next to me in my bedroom. I hear my phone vibrate. I know it is Pete. He is nudging me. "Fuck off," I mutter and close my eyes.

On the side of the tub is a lump of white Dove soap. I pick it up and begin washing, slowly letting the soap travel over my body.

When I get to my breasts, I feel a funny jag in the soap's progress over my left breast. I go back and try again. It happens once more, right where my chest meets the side of my breast, a little hop, skip, and jump. I drop the soap and let it float in the bubbly water like a little island in a warmed world. I bring my fingers to the spot, gently, cautiously. "Let's not go into this guns blazing," I tell myself.

"Oh my God," I say out loud. "This is a lump. Is it?" I feel again. Undeniably, there is a bump lodged under my skin. It is the size and shape of the small, hairy owl pellet we found last summer under our big white pine. It had mouse teeth and claws and feathers in it. But this, this is hard. And it feels sore around the edges; I can't move it or squish it. Underneath, I can feel my heart beating.

"Fuck." I look at the ceiling for what seems like a long time. Everything closes in and my cocoon feels like a prison now. I need to get out of the water. I need to breathe because suddenly I think I might be suffocating. Standing in the cold air, shivering,

I feel my breast once more. It is still there. This is no fluke of my mind. I feel so terribly alone I can't bear it and all I want is to have Pete there with me. Our years, these children, the months and weeks and small moments of time together, all come rushing back and there's this horrible virus, and this horrible woman, and yet still, right now, I want him here with me, helping me navigate, smiling and confident it will be okay.

Still wet, I go out to the living room and call. He picks up on the second ring.

"Pete. I—"

"Alice, I need to talk to you."

"I know, I—"

"Alice, I need to tell you something."

"So do I—I . . ."

"Alice, wait. I've been trying to have the time to talk to you with the kids asleep for weeks now. . . . It's not easy for me to tell you this—"

"Pete—"

"Alice, Goddammit—"

"Pete, you fucking asshole! Just shut up for a second. I found a fucking lump in my breast."

"A what?"

"A lump. In my breast."

"When?"

"I just found it. Now. Tonight. That's what I said."

"Is it big?"

"About the size of, I don't know, maybe a small rock or something. Bigger than a pebble. It's sort of oval-shaped. I've been so stressed and busy. I haven't been to my doctor for over a year now. I mean, I wasn't expecting. It could have been there for a while . . ." There's a long pause. We're both breathing into the phone like horses that have been cantering in the cold air. Then, he says, "I'm sorry. I'm so sorry, Alice. I've messed everything up. But I want to fix it. I want the chance." I hear a small but distinct sob catch in his throat. "Can I come home? Can I come be with you? I don't want to be without you anymore."

"But. Covid. And you've been in New York."

"Fuck Covid, Alice. I've been safe. I need to come back to Maine, now. I need my family."

I am standing in the living room, naked except for my towel. My legs and shoulders are still wet and I'm shivering. I can feel rivulets of water journeying down the inside of my thighs to soak into the rug below. What new country is this? I wonder. Nothing seems real or right. It's like we've slipped into a wrinkle in time we can't get out of, and it's full of danger everywhere I look. And Pete, my sweet, gorgeous, magnetic, flawed Pete, the Pete I'd like to kill and love all at the same time, is suddenly the only thing I can recognize in this storm.

"Alice. Can I come back to you? I can leave tonight." His voice is pleading.

There is only one answer that makes sense, one answer on the tip of my tongue. But instead of speaking, I look out at the white snow illuminated by the moon coming up over the woods where the girls and I were this afternoon. I want to wait a little longer until I am sure that when I utter it, I mean it.

# Author's Note

• • •

Alice appeared one evening in April of 2020, when I was downstairs by the fridge in the dark before bed. My husband was upstairs, the house was quiet. And her voice came to me. I knew immediately it was Alice, a character I dreamed up many years ago, but had not done anything with. Alice is a New Yorker with a second house in Maine. And now Alice wanted to come to Maine with her husband, Pete, to find refuge from the virus.

Since that March, as Covid descended, I had been concerned about people from away coming to Maine to buy up all the toilet paper, rent Airbnb's, or retreat to their second houses. I was worried they might take up all the hospital beds. Maine, where I was born and raised, is a poor and aging state. And, at least in our town, our grocery store was rationing toilet paper out of their back room to two rolls a family.

So, when Alice's voice appeared in my head, I told her to go away, I didn't have time—I was homeschooling my kids, for God's sake! And it was too complicated for me to understand her point of view. But she wouldn't leave. Suddenly I was writing a book about how privileged white people were coming to my vulnerable state. But as I humanized them, I realized that they also carried problems with them and were also seeking safety.

There's a joke in our family: When someone asks us how a trip or vacation was, we'll say, "It was great, but we took ourselves with us." I realized that Pete and Alice might have money and a nice car and a second house, but, like all of us, they bring themselves, too.

2020 was quite a year for my family: Shortly after Alice became my Ancient Mariner, my husband lost his job and went on unemployment. Then, in the fall, while we continued to homeschool our kids, I got sick from an autoimmune storm, likely triggered by a virus, which attacked my left eye, my thyroid, and then my pancreas. My eye and thyroid recovered, thankfully, but my pancreas did not. I was diagnosed in January of 2021 with autoimmune type-1 diabetes.

I am a child of divorce and, though I have been married now for fifteen years and have two sons, I can't say I know any better what magic recipe has so far kept my marriage intact. I am always surprised when some friends' marriages reach the breaking point when they seemed fixable, at least to me; and others that don't seem fixable stay together. Pete and Alice became a way for me to explore my questions on the page.

As I started writing from Alice's perspective, I found myself circling back to important questions I have had—increasingly—about my home state: Who gets to find sanctuary here? What happens to the natural world of Maine when many more people come? How will the influx of new people affect my Maine?

I wrote these pages like I was in a trance. I wrote around the edges of my health crisis, sheltering in place, homeschooling my kids, planning grocery budgets, and stressing about everything that was happening in our country and world. Funnily enough, Pete and Alice became a sort of refuge for *me*; a reprieve from my own life.

# Acknowledgments

● ● ●

It takes many experiences, lived, read, and imagined, all carefully filed away somewhere mysterious inside our psyches and bodies, to write a novel. For me, there are so many writers who have influenced me over the years. I could take a hundred pages here to list them all, starting with Shakespeare.

But, there were two writers' names on a yellow sticky note attached to my computer as I wrote *Pete and Alice in Maine*: John Updike and Elizabeth Strout. And under their names I wrote, "Caitlin, write what you know." I first met John Updike on the page when I was in college and read what I now believe is one of the best short stories ever written, "Separating." At the time, I was still reeling from my own parents' divorce. I pulled a quilt my mother had made for me over my head and wept. It was a profound, life-changing experience, to feel that there was another being out there who got the pain I felt and could put it down in such exquisite sentences. Later, I wrote about Updike in my thesis and, in that process, he and I corresponded. I interviewed him once for a show called *Studio 360* on WNYC, and we became pen-pal friendly. Later, when I had small children, I read *Anything Is Possible* by Elizabeth Strout. I'll never forget it: I finished the book, and went back to page one and started reading again, saying to myself, "How does she do this?" Over the next year, I read every single novel of hers, twice. I wanted to fall inside her world. I wanted to eat her sentences. Knowing that these two writers had come before me, could write with such integrity and honesty, could craft such poignant sentences, left me awestruck and gave me courage.

* * *

I could not have written this book without my two incandescent sons, M. & L. You two are the most exciting, interesting, brilliant people I have ever met. Every day is like Christmas: I get to unwrap a bit more of the gift that is you. I love you to pieces. Thank you for your patience while I took time to work; I could have been with you. It wasn't easy for me, either.

My husband, Dan: It was midnight, Covid year, May of 2020, and our kids were finally in bed and we'd done all our cleaning up for the next day. I read him the first chapter. "Oh my God," he said. "Read it again." Then, he said, "Stay here." He came back up with some cold white wine and two glasses and toasted me and then he disappeared downstairs. Because a friend had dropped off four oysters for us that very afternoon, he found a David Tanis recipe for fried oysters and cooked them for me. Sitting together in our kitchen we drank wine and ate the four oysters and he said, "Write the next part. I want to know what happens." For exactly a year he brought me breakfast and coffee before we homeschooled our kids in the mornings. He brought me big Ball jars of "gourmet water," which is ice water. He told me to keep going. Thank you, Dan.

There are two friends who were instrumental in the writing of this novel: My oldest and dearest friend, Craig Pospisil, a playwright, brilliant reader, master of snark and the quip that always makes me smile, who often understands me better than I do (or thinks he does). Craig read this book chapter by chapter and made it infinitely better. He kept me in it, kept me honest. And also my dear, lovely, Selina Rossiter, who read every draft of the book, generously, joyously, and then took the time to walk with me and discuss Pete and Alice in such incredible minutiae that they became real people for both of us. Thank you both for helping. As Selina once said, "It takes a village to raise a kid, raise a dog, have an old house, write a book." This could not be truer.

The following people read early drafts and gave me generous, enthusiastic, and important encouragement and notes: Glenn Harmon, Kathleen Sullivan, Debra Spark, Julie Fraize, Yael Reinharz, Merry Fogg, Rick Russo (thanks to Rick, Pete, a Connecticut boy, is no longer wearing a Red Sox T-shirt; unfortunately Pete likes the Yankees), Meredith Hall, Kate Christensen, Alice Elliott Dark, Susan Conley, Joanna Rakoff, Karen Karbo, Christina Baker Kline and Bill Roorbach.

# Acknowledgments

And thank you, once more, to Elizabeth Strout, a fellow Mainer and now, friend, who cheered me on as I wrote, and then read the book and cheered me on some more.

Thank you to later crucial reads by Roberta Zeff and Mary Pols, both of whom caught details that, when tweaked, made the book immeasurably better.

My computer guy, Stan Smith—my god, how many technical horrors have you, genius-man, fixed? How you find the irrecoverable in a sentence of gibberish code, I will never understand.

Friends who have gotten me through so much, your presence in the world tethers and soothes me: Andrea Meyer, Harlan and Aidan Bosmajian—I love you guys, you are family. Jodi Moger, Glenn and Fuchsia Harmon—family. I love you. Thank you to Sandy, Stuart, and Eloise Colhoun, husband, son, and daughter to Selina, you all inspired me by just being your wonderful selves.

My Frenchly team and family: Emmanuel Saint-Martin, Elisabeth Guédel, Emilie Assoun, Clément Mercet, Sophia Tamimy, Anne-Fleur Andrle, Cat Rickman, Karen Karbo, Kate Christensen, Debra Spark, Andrea Meyer, Philip Ruskin, Keith Van Sickle, Jana Misho. You all make the job a daily exploration. And you were so patient and encouraging with this novel thing. Thank you.

One's family of origin helps lays down the foundation that is the wellspring of every novel. My parents, Susan Hand Shetterly, and Robert Browne Shetterly Jr., have given me love, support, and friendship. Most importantly, my parents taught me to have high standards, to create with accuracy, to always strive for excellence. Thank you.

My uncle Jay has long supported me with encouragement at crucial moments and told me to keep going. He is also a terrific, generous reader. This adult relationship we have forged together is a great joy and source of comfort in my life. Thank you, Unca Jay. My aunt Maggie and my Uncle Eric are both two of my favorite people in the world and have given me much love, understanding, and encouragement over the years.

And finally, my Meme, Cherie Mason, great-grandmother to my boys, all around magical person. My youngest son said it best: "The only person as exciting as Santa is Meme." Not a day goes by when I don't think of her. She is missed—deeply and painfully—in our house. Yet I feel she is still with us.

Finally, no book comes into the world without a terrific team: Thank you, Lisa Grubka, my loyal, beyond-hard-working agent, always assiduous, consistently caring, incredible wordsmith. Thank you for trusting me when I said I was ready to take this book out to the world. And thank you to my brilliant, sharp, generous editor, Sarah Stein, who was way ahead of the pack, read the book and responded with such heart, there was nothing more to do but say "yes." Thank you to the entire team at Harper, including David Howe, Hayley Salmon, Joanne O'Neill, Katie O'Callaghan, Tracy Locke, Lydia Weaver, and Leah Carlson-Stanisic. Thank you all for taking me under your wing and guiding this book and me so expertly. I am forever grateful. You have made a novelist out of me.

# About the Author

● ● ●

CAITLIN SHETTERLY is the author of *Modified, Made for You and Me*, and the bestselling *Fault Lines: Stories of Divorce*. Her work has been featured in the *New York Times*, the *New York Times Magazine*, *Orion*, *Elle*, *Self*, and on Oprah.com, as well as on *This American Life* and various other public radio shows. She is the editor in chief of *Frenchly*, a French arts and culture online news magazine. A Maine native, she graduated with honors from Brown University and now lives with her two sons and husband in her home state. *Pete and Alice in Maine* is her first novel.